NORTHWEST
Reprints

Northwest Reprints
Series Editor: Robert J. Frank

Other titles in the series:

Beyond the Garden Gate
by Sophus K. Winther (introduction by Barbara Meldrum)

Botanical Exploration of the Trans-Mississippi West
by Susan Delano McKelvey (introduction by Stephen Dow Beckham)

Down in my Heart
by William Stafford (introduction by Kim Stafford)

Frontier Doctor
Urling C. Coe
Introduction by Robert Bunting

Happy Valley
by Anne Shannon Monroe (introduction by Karen Blair)

A Homesteader's Portfolio
by Alice Day Pratt (introduction by Molly Gloss)

The Land Is Bright
by Archie Binns (introduction by Ann Ronald)

Nehalem Tillamook Tales
told by Clara Pearson, collected by Elizabeth Jacobs (introduction by Jarold Ramsey)

On the Highest Hill
by Roderick Haig-Brown (introduction by Laurie Ricou)

Oregon Detour
by Nard Jones (introduction by George Venn)

Requiem for a People: The Rogue Indians and the Frontiersmen
by Stephen Dow Beckham (with a new introduction by the author)

Timber
by Roderick Haig-Brown (introduction by Glen A. Love)

The Viewless Winds
by Murray Morgan (introduction by Harold Simonson)

Wildmen, Wobblies & Whistle Punks: Stewart Holbrook's Lowbrow Northwest
(edited and introduced by Brian Booth)

Yamsi: A Year in the Life of a Wilderness Ranch
by Dayton O. Hyde (introduction by William Kittredge)

Tall Tales from Rogue River

The Yarns of Hathaway Jones

Edited by Stephen Dow Beckham
Illustrations by Christina Romano

Oregon State University Press
Corvallis Oregon

The paper in this book meets the guidelines for permanence and durability of the Committee on Production Guidelines for Book Longevity of the Council on Library Resources and the minimum requirements of the American National Standard for Permanence of Paper for Printed Library Materials Z39.48-1984.

Library of Congress Cataloging-in-Publication Data
Jones, Hathaway, 1878-1937
    Tall tales from Rogue river : the yarns of Hathaway Jones / edited by Stephen Dow Beckham ; illustrations by Christina Romano.
        p. cm. — (Northwest reprints)
    Includes bibliographical references.
    ISBN 0-87071-512-7
    1. Tales—Oregon—Rogue River Valley. I. Beckham, Stephen Dow. II. Romano, Christina. III. Title. IV. Series.
GR110.07J64 1991
398.2'0979521—dc20   9041875
                                                                            CIP

Oregon State University Press
101 Waldo Hall
Corvallis OR 97331-6407
541-737-3166 •fax 541-737-3170
osu.orst.edu/dept/press

Preface

> *but there were things*
> *That covered what a man was, and set him apart*
> *From others, things by which others knew him. The place*
> *Where he lived, the horse he rode, his relatives, his wife.*
> *His voice, complexion, beard, politics, religion or lack of it,*
> *And so on. With time, these things fall away*
> *Or dwindle into shadows: river sand blowing away*
> *From some ling-buried old structure of bleached boards*
> *That appears a vague shadow through the sand-haze,*
> > *and then stands clear,*
> *Naked, angular, itself.*
>
> > –from "Trial and Error," H.L. Davis

People new to a region are especially interested in what things might set them apart from others. In works by northwest writers, we get to know about out history and culture, and about our flora and fauna. And with time, some things about ourselves start to come into focus out of the shadows of our history.

To give readers an opportunity to look into the place where Northwesterners live, the Oregon State University Press is making available again many books that are out of print. The Northwest Reprint Series will reissue a range of books, both fiction and nonfiction. Books will be selected for different reasons: some for their literary merit, some for their historical significance, some for provocative concerns, and some for these and other reasons together. Foremost, however, will be the book's potential to interest a range of readers who are curious about the region's voice and complexion. The Northwest Reprint Series will make works of well-known and lesser-known writers available for all.

–RJF

NORTHWEST
Reprints

Tall Tales

FROM

Rogue River

The Yarns

OF

Hathaway Jones

Edited by STEPHEN DOW BECKHAM

Illustrations by Christina Romano

INDIANA UNIVERSITY PRESS
Bloomington / London

For
CURT BECKHAM
Master Yarn-Spinner

CONTENTS

CONTENTS

CONTENTS

PREFACE

Southwest Oregon possesses a ruggedness that makes it a last frontier. Hathaway Jones, a product of that region, captured much of its beauties and dangers in the matchless tales that he wove and recounted during the decades that he made his solitary trek of the canyon of the Rogue River as a mule-team mail carrier. The pungent place names, tranquil forest glens, and rushing cascades of river cutting stone not only helped Hathaway's imagination but today have become sights that draw world-weary city-dwellers on foot and in boats into that same awesome stretch of mountain wilderness.

The presence of Hathaway Jones first came to me more than two decades ago when I, too, became enchanted with the Rogue country. His adventures and tragic death became all too real when, hiking near the Big Bend of the Rogue River one spring day, I climbed a small hill to find a crude tombstone that bore his name. Although Jones has been dead nearly forty years, his stories are still alive in the wilds of Oregon. This book represents only that part of Hathaway's repertoire that drifted into my net.

As a fisherman in folklore I have had many helpers. I thank Professor J. Barre Toelken of the University of Oregon for his counsel and encouragement over a number of years. I am obliged to David Duniway, former state archivist of Oregon, for his assistance in consulting the WPA Oregon folklore materials. I am also indebted to Martin Schmitt and Glenda Kupper of the Department of Special Collections of the University of Oregon.

My oral informants who brought Hathaway to life so vividly were graciously cooperative. I thank Larry Lucas, Sam Baer, Ed Troyer, Loson Winn, John Pettinger, Mabel Lucas Butler, and Mary Reitsma. The late Alice Wooldridge kindly assisted in interviewing Hathaway's friends of many years, Charles and Sadie Pettinger, before their deaths. To Curtis Beckham I am grateful for his work with Todd Jones, Hathaway's last surviving brother. I also thank Addie Fitzhugh Helmkin, Dorice Baer, George Abdill, Wallace Wade, Eugene and Dorothy Marsh, and my parents, Dow and Anna Beckham, for their assistance.

Christina Romano, the illustrator, has generously responded to the needs of this project and has captured in her own remarkable style the spirit of the Jones tales.

Lastly I thank my wife Patti for her patient encouragement throughout the days and weeks of labor on this book.

McMinnville, Oregon   Stephen Dow Beckham

Tall Tales from Rogue River

The Münchausen of the Rogue

The spinner of tall tales was for centuries a familiar figure in human society. In the pre-electronic media era, oral recounting of adventures, dreams, aspirations, fears, and folklore occupied a very significant part of man's life. Without the entertainment of radio and television and without electric lights to encourage reading, men and women possessed the luxury of a tale-telling society. They lived in a world of *Märchen,* whoppers or "windies," anecdotes, and jests. While folk genre persist in superstitions, jokes, ballads, anecdotes, and tales, the noncommercial raconteur of *Märchen* and Münchausen tales has become much rarer.

When regional Münchausens do appear, they are as likely to be pounced upon by eager folklorists as by the P.T.A. wanting a program speaker. That such a figure as a teller of tall tales could flourish for the first four decades of the twentieth century, miss literally every electronic media influence, and thrive in a world where the inventions of modern man had negligible influence is indeed unusual.

Hathaway Jones was no usual man. A regional Münchausen of remarkable talents, he lived well insulated from society. Jones very aptly fulfilled Jan Brunvand's identification of such a figure:

> The typical hero of *genuine* oral tradition in the United States is not the brawling frontier trailblazer or the giant mythical

laborer, but rather the local tall-tale specialist who has gathered a repertoire of traditional exaggerations and attached them all to his own career.[1]

Jones and his stories are inextricably linked to the Rogue country, a mountain wilderness that surrounds the hundred-mile-long canyon of the Rogue River in southwestern Oregon. Rising near the base of Mount Mazama, the extinct volcano that holds Crater Lake, the Rogue River flows from the Cascades into the Rogue Valley before beginning its wild dash to the sea. Its course to the west, a route that was the homeland of Hathaway Jones, is a tortuous region of precipitous cliffs, narrow river bends, virgin forests, and the solitude of the Siskiyou Mountains. The earthy geographical nomenclature of the river's run—Hell's Gate, Solitude Bar, Paradise Bar, Horseshoe Bend, Battle Bar, Whiskey Creek, and Nail Keg Riffle—testify to its character.

This land was first penetrated by white men in 1851. For at least five centuries it had been the domain of the Shasta Coasta and the Tututni Indians, a race of resilient Athapascan-speakers who had turned west to settle near the Pacific Ocean during their long trek down the North American continent. The region's written history was born in violence, for, as gold-crazed miners rushed into the Rogue River watershed in the early 1850's, they wantonly massacred the people who lived on the banks of the river. The Rogue Indians fought back. In 1853 and again in 1855–56 wars convulsed the region and ended only in the defeat of the Indians and their removal to a distant reservation nearly 200 miles up the Oregon coast.[2]

In the fall of 1853, as pioneers rushed to Oregon to file for free lands under the Donation Land Act, Hathaway Jones's forebears settled in Douglas County. They located in the upper part of the argiculturally rich Umpqua Valley immediately north of the Rogue River wilderness. His grandfather, who became the central figure in a cycle of Jones's Münchausen tales, was Isaac Jones. Born October 22, 1816, in Morgan County, Ohio, Jones brought his wife, Anna, and several children overland to Oregon Territory in 1852. They took a claim of 320 acres on Deer Creek on November 25, 1854.[3] Isaac Jones built the Roseburg Flouring Mills and operated them for many years. He died on December 7, 1893, at the residence of Thompson Criteser, his son-in-law, in Roseburg, Oregon.[4]

Among the four sons and three daughters who survived him was William Sampson Jones, the father of Hathaway. Born August 16, 1841, in Indiana, William Jones had come to Oregon as a boy of twelve. About 1863 he married Elizabeth Leuserbia Epperson. She had emigrated to Oregon with her parents from Iowa, having been born there on February 5, 1842. Before their divorce in 1883, William and Elizabeth Jones became the parents of eight children. Hathaway, born October 28, 1870, was their third child and third son.[5]

For many years William Jones was a bartender in Rose-burg, the county seat of Douglas County. Shortly after his wife left him and remarried, however, he decided to become a miner. Although the life in the diggings was lonely, it appealed to men who wanted to turn away from society. In 1890 Jones and his son Hathaway left Roseburg and journeyed into the Siskiyou Mountains where they began mining on the East Fork of Mule Creek. They worked the claim for two summers then selected another at Battle Bar, five miles up the Rogue River from Marial.[6]

Battle Bar, site of one of the hostile engagements of Indians and soldiers in 1855, was the home of William Sampson Jones until the 1920's. The bar is located at a gentle bend in the river opposite a ridge of a thousand feet on which groves of tanbark oak and meadows of grass meander down to the stream banks. In that isolated region—some forty arduous pack miles by trail from the Oregon–California railroad and even farther from "civilization"—Hathaway Jones became a famed teller of tall tales.

One of the earliest accounts of him and of his Münchausen feats was written by Claude Riddle and concerned Riddle's mining ventures in the Rogue Canyon in 1903. Expecting Hathaway to help him and his partner pack supplies down the canyon, Riddle recalled:

> We were busy assembling our outfit, when we heard the jangle of bells and the scuffle of horses' feet on the trail. Some unintelligible human calls were heard from the approaching cavalcade. It was Hathaway directing his animals. The file of horses and mules meandered down from the trail to the flat where we had our camp, and Hathaway appeared in person.
>
> He was small and short and walked with a forward stoop. His arms were long and his hands seemed to swing ahead below his knees. Later I saw him in profile walking up a hill, taking such long steps that his body bobbed up and down, giving the impression that he was walking on four legs. He wore a conical little black hat with a buckskin string woven in for a headband. His heavy blue flannel shirt was open and black hair decorated his throat and breast. A narrow leather

belt held his pants about his slim hips and it looked like he
might come apart in the middle at any time. Hathaway's
speech was most peculiar—a cross between a hairlip and
tonguetie. His pronunciation of some words was intriguing,
and he always seemed in dead earnest.[7]

On that mining expedition Riddle met Jones for the only
time. So memorable were the tales and his images of their
teller, however, that when he wrote his reminiscences in 1954,
Riddle yet recalled a dozen of the yarns in detail.[8]

The Rogue River wilderness underwent a minor mining
boom in the years immediately before Hathaway and his
father settled in the region. A hardy few miners had settled at
the Big Bend of the Rogue in the mid-1850's. In 1863 prospectors filed on copper and quartz claims near the Devil's Backbone about eight miles from Big Bend.[9] By 1885 ambitious
hydraulic mining projects reached a climax in the upriver
canyons. Building ditches that took backbreaking labor,
William Day and John Fitzhugh washed the sands of Solitude
Bar that year; other men labored at Blossom Bar, Douglas Bar,
and Walker Bar.[10]

These men helped build the trails that opened part of the
Rogue country. Some of them floated equipment down the
Rogue River; others carried it by pack animal from the Oregon
and California railroad. The rail line, pushed south from
Roseburg, reached Ashland in the Rogue River Valley in May,
1884.[11] In the 1890's, realizing that the rail service passed the
upper end of Rogue country, coastal Curry County residents
—particularly those who lived at Gold Beach at the river's
mouth—began to think about establishing a mail route to the
interior. Gold Beach, the county seat, was situated at a dan-

[7]

gerous fair-weather harbor. The rugged coast mountains made travel slow and often impossible. Only rude trails connected Gold Beach with Crescent City on the coast to the south or with Port Orford nearly thirty miles north.

The thinking, planning, and successful lobbying of the residents of the lower Rogue eventually led to the establishment of a U.S. mail route from West Fork (Dothan Post Office) in the Cow Creek Canyon of the Umpqua watershed to Gold Beach. The line went from the railhead up the West Fork of Cow Creek, over the mountains into the headwaters of Mule Creek, and down that stream to the cabins at its mouth. It then led by trail down the Rogue River to Illahe at the Big Bend and on to Agness at the forks of the Illinois and the Rogue. It then went by trail over the mountains to the coast. At the turn of the century, however, a boat line contract was established to carry the mail the last forty miles to the ocean.[12]

In 1898 Hathaway Jones became a contract mail carrier on the eastern end of the route. Responsible for the Dothan to Illahe section, he continued this solitary employment with occasional special packing contracts like that with Riddle until 1937. During those years he married Flora Thomas, whose parents had homesteaded about three miles upriver from Illahe. They had a son and a daughter before Flora left Jones for another man. When his father became too old to remain at Battle Bar, he also left the Rogue River and resided with a son, Richard Jones, until his death of cancer in the 1920's in Portland, Oregon.[13]

In spite of his family misfortunes, Hathaway loved the wilds of the Rogue River. At Illahe he resided with the Charles Pettinger family at Big Bend Ranch. He loaded his mules and

[8]

year after year trekked up and down the narrow trails that led him to Flora Dell, Brushy Bar, Burns Creek, and Marial, the post office established in 1903 at the mouth of Mule Creek. He carried tools, letters, mail order clothing, and new catalogues to the scattered miners and hardy few families who eked out an existence in the Rogue wilderness by hunting, fishing, mining, and peeling the tanbark from the oaks to sell to dealers for leather processing.[14]

To these people Hathaway Jones represented the outside world. His horizons were wider than theirs and his journeys up and down the river introduced him to the latest gossip, the first news of tragedy, and the tenor of life on that rugged frontier. Plagued with a noticeable harelip and cleft palate, Jones spoke with an unusual twang and hesitation. His rendering of "small talk" received unexpected embellishment merely through his telling it in his own remarkable style. Further, his solitary days and nights on the trail gave him more than ample opportunity to develop a humorous twist to a commonplace event.

Emerging from a world of vocal entertainment and living fully within that world all of his sixty-seven years, Jones early gained a reputation as a Münchausen. In this regard he only partially fit Richard M. Dorson's description of tellers of tall tales, for Dorson wrote in 1959: "Obscure and humbly born, the Münchausens never attract public notice, but occasionally they drift into the net of folklore collectors."[15] In Jones's case the folklorists did not ensnare him; the public did.

The Rogue River Canyon drew outsiders as occasional visitors. Some like Zane Grey became so enamored with the remoteness of that country that they annually came to fish the

[9]

riffles of the Rogue for steelhead and salmon. Although few of these fishermen–sportsmen met Jones, he had become a familiar object of conversation the length of the river. Guides, miners, packers, and settlers told and retold his tales and helped create a "reputation" that, with the passage of time, became very important to Jones. Nancy Wilson Ross, who rode the mail boat from Gold Beach to Agness in the summer of 1940, collected a few of Jones's stories and noted:

> Hathaway was proud of the distinction of being the biggest liar in the country, and, on hearing once that the Portland *Oregonian* had bestowed the honor on someone else, threatened to institute suit against the paper.[16]

For Hathaway Jones, telling tales provided an entry into the rough-and-tumble society along the river. A humble man who grew a bushy mustache to hide his harelip, Jones undoubtedly discovered early in life that his keen wit and fabricated adventures brought a chuckle to his associates and an acceptance to himself. That his stature was well established was evidenced by the news articles of his tragic death. The *Oregonian,* that newspaper he had threatened to sue, carried a moving obituary of him in 1937. Entitled "A Hillman Named Hathaway Jones," it recounted his accidental death—thrown from his mule into a rocky gorge above Illahe—and speculated on his life:

> The story which tells of the passing of Hathaway Jones presents him as being distinctly a character, with a shrewd and merry wit. Now here is a problem: do the far silent places shape such men, or do such men seek out the remote canyons to build their cabins back of beyond? Lord, how we envy them

sometimes, these fellows like Hathaway Jones, who seem to have soaked up the very flavor of the firs or the prairies. The sea has that way with some men, too. It is evident that living in towns and belonging to literary societies, or luncheon clubs and lodges, somehow doesn't do half so much for us as the Rogue river canyon does for such men as Hathaway Jones. Somehow they seem to have been going to school all the time, by themselves, at some sort of college. And maybe they have.

You never knew a business man, for example, who wasn't flattered when a man like Hathaway Jones took a fancy to him, and gave him his friendship, somewhere out back of beyond, over a tin cup of muddy coffee and a tin pan of burned bacon. Sitting there, looking across the fire at a man like Hathaway Jones, and admiring him, and envying him, and listening to every word he had to say. But you see how it is—if all of us became ambitious to be like Hathaway Jones, and went into the canyons to be alone with ourselves, it wouldn't be any time at all until there would be half a dozen filling stations on the west fork, with as many sandwich shops and an auto camp, and the deer would be over the mountains. And so, by the way, would be Hathaway Jones, or whatever you called him.

After a bit, now that Hathaway Jones is gone, the recollections that folks have of him will become dim, and the dimness will increase to legendry, and then the very legend of him will be disremembered as though he had never been. But the forest will be there, and the canyon, or somewhere else—it doesn't matter—and when you come to a place where the rough road dwindles down to a trail, all you'll have to do is to follow the trail to its spit-and-image of Hathaway Jones lounging out of a cabin to greet you. It's true enough they'll call him something else, but there he'll be. And then he'll put the coffee on.[17]

Like other Münchausens, Jones wove a set of stories that revolved around his own adventures in his immediate setting

—the Rogue River wilderness. Unlike some of these tall-tale tellers, however, he also developed cycles that included his father, William Sampson Jones, and his grandfather, Isaac Jones. As if to enhance his own stature, he emphasized the Sampson in his father's name and endowed the old man with strength, having him nursed in infancy in one tale by a panther. His grandfather, Ike, became the wise old man of the woods, who, often as not, had tame animal friends that made life more simple and comfortable for him.

Mody Boatright developed a number of years ago the thesis that Münchausen tales could be seen as a variety of reverse bragging. The incredible hardships and dangers of the frontier, the stark reality of death, and the exuberant re-action of those who settled in the wilds to the dude's image of those conditions—these things, in Boatright's opinion, in-fluenced the course of the tall tale. The yarn-spinner laughed at the harsh realities.[18] That Jones did so is most apparent. His encounters with rattlesnakes, bears, rolling stones, pre-cipitous cliffs, and snowstorms—common features in his tales—were all too much a part of his life on the Rogue River. The seriousness of these threats to his existence he shoved aside as he bragged in his stories how he met, outwitted, and conquered these obstacles.

In spite of his isolation from the outside world, Jones un-doubtedly acquired tales or tale motifs from others. He lived his first twenty years in the close society of the Jones clan in Douglas County. At West Fork, occasionally in Glendale or Canyonville, and in Gold Beach once or twice each year, Jones usually visited the saloons and there swapped yarns and defended his reputation as the "damnedest liar in the state."

His skill as a raconteur, however, was in his matchless ability to recreate familiar tale elements in the garb and setting of the Rogue country. He gave his stories a plausibilty and a delivery that made them, at once, yarns of his own.

The identification of such motifs as "shoe pegs sold for oats" (X1821*), "remarkable ammunition used by great hunter" (X1759*(gd)), "dog with remarkable scent" (X1214.10), and "man bores holes in tree trunk, fills them with honey, hangs heavy stone in front of holes; bear pushes rock away to get at honey; the rock hits him in head . . . " (X1124(d)) indicate that Jones was adept at reworking old tales. Never, however, did he indicate that his repertoire was anything other than his own creation. To have done so would have violated his own uncanny deadpan delivery and immediately reduced him from the center of action to merely being a teller of tales. Although he did not personally figure in the tale cycles about his father or grandfather, Hathaway Jones became the vicarious inheritor of these tales' focus as the flesh-and-blood grandson of old Ike or the son of Sampson Jones.

The Jones tales are remarkably simple and straightforward. Although some latter-day spinners of the yarns have embellished them with phrases that probably make Hathaway "flip-flop backwards" in his grave, to use his expression, all indications are that the original renditions were neither lengthy nor complicated. Arthur Dorn, collector of the largest number of Jones's yarns, gave them, however, considerably more polish and literary expression than they usually received. Jones did not employ the yarn-spinner's device of the "traveler's tale" nor did he use a "mysterious informant." He did, however, sometimes use the "catch tale" and led to the punch line in a yarn by setting himself up for an interruption that at once enabled him to deliver the tale's *coup de grace.*

Jones's repertoire reveals that he lived in a world of men. His tales are exclusively masculine except on rare occasions and, in those cases, the women are merely the backdrop to the real interest in the anecdotal account. Further, the men in the tales, as in life, were drinkers of "moon" and, at times, "hard cases." As with Len Henry of Idaho, John Darling of New York, or Gib Morgan of the oil fields, the life of the Münchausen was one of masculine deeds and daring.

Metaphor was Jones's strong suit. His use of it was always lively and pungent. One of his most memorable phrases, which on reflection is quite nonsensical, was the assertion that something was "makin' more noise than drivin' a four-horse team through the woods draggin' a bull-hide."[19] So complicated was the phrase that listeners were at once convinced that Jones had aptly described a staggering event.

He also employed a set of vivid if somewhat peculiar phrases at any tense or necessary moment. They included: "get on with your rat killin'," "independent as a hog on ice," "puffin' like a bay steer," "meaner than cat dung," "the still sow gets the swill," and "stingier than boiled owl droppings." Sometimes Hathaway proclaimed that it was time to "get up and dust"; he was clearing out. To remind a nosey outsider to mind his own business, he said: "Don't mix in other people's bear fights." And if something happened fast, it was "quicker than chained lightning," which had to be fast since Jones claimed that he could run right up lightning, pull it up after him, and float down on the thunder.[20]

Understatement was another technique that Jones used with skill. Once when asked how he had received his speech impediment, he reportedly said that he had quarreled with his Pa and that the old man had hit him in the nose with a shovel. "This was what caused the trouble," insisted Hathaway. Then to clinch it, he added that his Pa was older than he was at the time.[21]

Claude Riddle recalled another example:

> One day he [Hathaway] was looking at the bead on my gun
> and he said a bead didn't do much good when you were hunting
> bear. He said, "When you get to fightin' a bear hand to hand,
> and stick your gun muzzle in the bear's mouth, about half the
> time he will bite the bead off anyhow.[22]

On the trail, in camp, wherever he was, Hathaway had a ready comment for the situation. Glen Wooldridge, veteran river guide from Grants Pass, described Jones as "lank, in fact, so stretched out it was hard to tell anything about him. But he could think up a tall story faster than a dog can trot."[23] On the packing trip in 1903, Hathaway turned to Riddle as the men were getting their packs on the animals:

> "Now this little bay mule, Dandy," he said, "he's one of the
> best I've got. He can carry a pack just as careful, never bumps
> trees or anything, but he gets stubborn streaks when I can
> hardly do anything with him. He just won't do nothin'.
> Stubbornest thing I ever saw. He's stubborn as a damn mule."[24]

As a yarn-spinner Jones knew the value of circumstantial detail. He threw in tidbits about the weather, the size and heights of trees, place names, and even dates to add plausibility to his story. He built each account logically and saved the less-than-expected ending for just the right moment. Speaking of such a raconteur in general, Mody Boatright could well have been describing Hathaway Jones when he wrote:

> He knew that he must provide ludicrous imagery, an ingenious piling up of epithets, a sudden transition, a non sequitur—something besides mere exaggeration if his audience was to respond to his tales.[25]

None of the surviving Jones repertoire are tales of humor about sex. Those who knew him well have not dwelt on ribald anecdotes or recalled yarns with sexual overtones. When queried about Hathaway, Sadie and Charles Pettinger, his close friends of more than forty years, were tight-lipped. The interviewer wrote:

> They wouldn't talk; said he was a nice old man and all the funny remarks he made were about himself or something that happened to him. They were afraid that people would ridicule him and they said he never said anything about other people.[26]

Others, however, in anecdotal accounts, stress that Jones's full repertoire was not for "parlor company."[27]

While informants remember Jones's tales, they recall virtually nothing about his personal life. His journey into legendry had begun before his death and grew quickly thereafter. The Oregonian obituary notice said: "Born in Roseburg, Hathaway had lived at Big Bend Ranch on the Rogue longer than anyone there remembers. . . . No survivors are known."[28]

Nancy Wilson Ross, who collected his tales during a visit at Agness, wrote in 1941:

> One cannot really imagine Hathaway Jones emerging from any other kind of country; fabulous Hathaway with his unknown antecedents, his cleft palate, his mysterious and terrible death, whose imaginary exploits illustrating his own courage, strength, and ingenuity have made him one of the immortal yarners of the Pacific Northwest.[29]

Jones, while the best-known of the tale-spinners of the Rogue River, was not the only Münchausen in the area. John Fitzhugh, the pseudonymous EKOMS in Curry County newspapers at the turn of the century, was both a raconteur of tall tales and a ballad singer. Although his songs such as "The Beckoning Hand" have almost been entirely forgotten, his tales were recounted as late as the 1930's.[30]

Like Jones, Fitzhugh was a member of a pioneer family in Douglas County. His father, Solomon Fitzhugh, brought his wife and children to Oregon in 1851. John Fitzhugh first entered the Rogue country in 1855–56 when he served as a volunteer soldier in the Rogue Indian wars. By the 1880's he had settled deep in the wilderness, locating in the upriver canyons a decade before Sampson and Hathaway Jones came to the region as miners. Fitzhugh named his home Solitude and there he mined with his brother-in-law William P. Day of Camas Valley. After ten years of work at Solitude Bar, Fitzhugh moved to the upper part of Sixes River in northern Curry County. There he hunted bear, played the guitar and harmonica, and sang to his many nieces and nephews. Fitzhugh died July 6, 1903, in Langlois, Oregon.[31]

The kinship of Fitzhugh's tales to those of Hathaway Jones

is revealed in two recalled in October, 1938, by Fred S. Moore of Gold Beach. Remembering them as EKOMS yarns published about 1900 in the Port Orford *Tribune,* Moore began:

> John Fitzhugh was mining at Illahe and he decided to go hunting as meat was getting scarce. His shoes had worn out so he went barefooted. He hadn't been gone long when he noticed what he took to be a huge bear track.
>
> Well he tracked that bear the biggest part of the day. Finally he noticed a track he had just made himself and found he had been tracking himself all this time. He said: "I don't know what would have happened if I had met myself as I happened to be a pretty good shot."

The other yarn also had a Rogue River Canyon setting:

> Fitzhugh sent to Gold Beach for a pair of Gum boots, size eight. As the stock of boots were [sic] low just then the nearest they could come to filling his order was size nine.
>
> One day the store received a letter saying that he had received the boots all right and worn them. But the first day he had worn them he had gone to a claim over a ridge near by. He went up all right but on the way back after he got halfway down the ridge he suddenly found he could go no farther. He was quite puzzled, and finally discovered that the heels were caught on the ridge.[32]

John Fry, a man who was a frequent spinner of Hathaway Jones's tales, also developed a number of his own. Fry's family came to the Rogue River in 1867 and 1868. His uncle, James Fry, a miner from Fry Town, Iowa, settled in October, 1867, at Oak Flats on the lower Illinois River, a tributary of the Rogue. The following year John's father, Abraham Fry, also came to the Rogue Canyon. The brothers and their mining partner John Billings had all taken Indian wives while living in the diggings near Yreka on the mid-section of the Klamath River. Before coming to the Rogue, Abraham Fry had served as a packer on the trails between the mines and the small harbor at Crescent City, California.[33]

John Fry, born May 10, 1861, thus had strong ties to the mining frontier and to one of the wildest sections of the Far West. From his mother's family he inherited a legacy of long association with the region—his grandmother was a shaman among her people. Although isolated in part from that culture —his father abandoned his mother for another Indian wife before he came to the Rogue—John Fry knew the Indian life because he lived for several years at the Siletz Reservation before returning to Agness to make his home. He died on Rogue River in 1946. Fry's tales, while set in the Rogue country, do not show the development of the Jones genre.[34] They were sufficiently popular, however, to gain him a reputation along the river.

It was a lonely homeland in which Hathaway Jones, John Fry, John Fitzhugh, and the other early settlers swapped yarns and confronted nature. In 1900 Curry County, running for fifty-five miles along the southern Oregon coast, had a population of 1,868 people. Most of them lived near the shore; few penetrated the heavily forested mountains or tortuous river canyons. By 1930, though it had 3,257 inhabitants, the county possessed no incorporated towns. Throughout Jones's lifetime the region was the "far country."[35]

Sparse as was the settlement, the hills and canyons of the Rogue were clearly defined territory. They had not been recorded on the topographers' maps, but men had left their mark.

[19]

Describing the area at the forks of the Illinois and Rogue rivers in the 1930's, Arthur Dorn noted:

> South and west of the Illinois is the hunting ground of the John and Ike Fry outfit; Burned Ridge, High Ridge, and east to Bear Camp belongs to the Blondells; north of the Rogue, including Lake of the Woods, Brushy Mountain, and out to Iron Mountain, belongs to the Cooley–Lucas family; all the Illahe country belongs to the Billings outfit, while Silver Peak, Bob's Garden, Brandy Peak, and Squirrel Camp, are reserved for private hunting by all natives when not accompanied with "dude sports."[36]

That wilderness region became the final resting place of Hathaway Jones. His grave is atop a small hill covered with oaks and firs looking over the Big Bend of the Rogue and into the mountains of the upriver country. A simple man, an honest man, Hathaway Jones was a spinner of yarns and a bringer of warmth to those who knew him or heard of his adventures.

The Informants

Hathaway Jones's stories have appeared in travel books, the *Saturday Evening Post*, the WPA Writer's Project guide to Oregon, newspapers, and in local history publications. Arthur Dorn collected the greatest part of the repertoire between 1936 and 1941 in preparation for the never-completed Oregon Folklore Project of the WPA. A former San Francisco attorney who was a frequent sportsman on the Rogue, Dorn and his wife retreated to a hillside cabin near Agness during the depression. In that Shangri-la they fished, hunted, tended a vegetable garden, and translated the sutras. Whenever possible, Dorn made notes on the folklore of the region. His labors were not published.

In almost every tale he collected, Dorn rendered the account to third person. He eliminated Hathaway's inimitable dialect, and though his collection thus creates a "distance" from Jones's delivery, it is an extremely significant compilation because of its size, its exacting detail, and its "contemporary" nature. Many of the tales Dorn collected from Hathaway or recorded them during Jones's lifetime. The Dorn collection preserves many of the specific elements of the yarns that have been forgotten by latter-day raconteurs.

Dorn's informants not only included Jones but also John Fry, Larry Lucas, Rolly Canfield, Claude Bardin, Lin Blondell, and Andrew J. Hatfield. These men were all long-time residents along the river, most of them residing in the Agness-Illahe area. Occasionally serving as guides and often passing the lazy days of summer on a porch or doorstep of a cabin along the river, they told and retold the Jones tales and enabled Dorn to accumulate a representative collection of the yarns.

Larry Lucas, proprietor of the hotel-lodge at Agness for more than forty years, is probably the best-versed raconteur of Jones's tales. Lucas came to Agness in 1902. While his father, Marcellus Lucas was alive, the family lived at Shasta Coasta Creek, a small tributary of the Rogue between Agness and Illahe. After his mother, Sadie, married Charles Pettinger, the family settled at the Big Bend Ranch near Illahe. Pettinger held the mail contracts under which Hathaway was a carrier for nearly thirty-five years. Jones boarded with the Pettingers and there Lucas learned how to conjure up Hathaway's nasal twang and hesitating speech.

Claude Bardin, another of Dorn's informants, resided at Two Mile Riffle below Illahe. A veteran of World War I, Bardin was born in Oregon in 1879 and settled on Rogue River in 1890. He was a trapper and guide on the river between Grants Pass and the ocean and knew Hathaway for fifty years. Similarly Andrew J. Hatfield was an old-timer on the river. Born in a wagon on the plains in June, 1851, Hatfield came to the Rogue with his father shortly after the closing of the Indian wars in 1856. Hatfield was a bachelor and a rather lonely old man when Dorn visited his log cabin to collect Jones's tales in 1941.

Lin Blondell, who has long lived at the forks of the Rogue

and Illinois rivers at Agness, came to the region in the fall of 1917. His father brought him and several other children to the former Merriman Ranch, a property the Blondells have farmed for many years. Dorn identified the Blondell place as the site of Dogwood Park, the location of the wild Fourth of July celebrations of the 1880's recounted in the tale of the "Wild Hog Derby."

Loson Winn of Canyonville, Oregon, is another well-informed tale-spinner. With his wife Mexia, Winn has operated a small pie shop for forty-five years in the lonely canyon where the highway to California snakes over the Umpqua Mountains. He has picked up the Jones tales on the West Fork or Dothan end of the mail route.

Sam Baer and Ed Troyer, a cousin of Winn, are also familiar with part of the Jones repertoire. Both residents of Coos Bay, Oregon, they learned the tales on hunting and fishing trips to Rogue River. Baer's father, the late Charles Baer, delighted in telling the Jones stories. Isaac R. Tower of North Bend, Oregon, was another Rogue River angler who knew many of the yarns.

Claude Riddle, born in 1877, collected his Jones tales during the packing trip with Hathaway in 1903 and through a lifetime residence in the Cow Creek Valley. Jean Muir, whose article carried two of the Jones stories in the *Saturday Evening Post* in 1946, heard them from Glen Wooldridge, veteran Rogue River guide out of Grants Pass. Nancy Wilson Ross's accounts of Hathaway in *Farthest Reach,* her travel book about the Pacific Northwest, were obtained during a visit with Arthur Dorn shortly before World War II. Similarly the Jones's stories published by Kathryn McPherson in the newspaper supplement, *Oregon's South Coast,* in 1960, were gleaned in part from Dorn's notes.

Former President of the Oregon Senate, Eugene Marsh, and his wife Dorothy, remember some of the Jones tales heard during fishing trips to the Rogue. Among their favorites, which is recalled only in fragment, is the familiar motif wherein Hathaway, in order to save a farm wagon, had to amputate the wagon's tongue. It had been bitten by a rattlesnake.

Linda Barker collected a series of anecdotes and a few tales of Jones in the mid-1960's. The accounts were by Joel Barker of Grants Pass, Oregon. Her manuscript in the Randall V. Mills Folklore Archive of the University of Oregon reveals the journey of Jones into legend. Barker was unable to provide any concrete biographical details about Hathaway. Some of what he did recount was "tall tale" itself.

The viability of Hathaway Jones's yarns is attested by the popularity they hold nearly forty years after his death. Along the Rogue River, in distant cities and towns, at family gatherings—in a variety of places—one yet hears the tall tales of the Münchausen of the Rogue.

Ike Jones and the Smart Bear

"Maybe," suggested Hathaway, "I had ought to put bears ahead of mules for smartness, only some bears don't seem to be smart, while mules are all highly intelligent."

He then told them about the fall his granddad, Ike, went out to Grants Pass and stayed until the following spring. Old Ike thought he had liver complaint, but it turned out to be sour stomach brought on by too much wild hog and moonshine.

Before going outside for the winter, Ike husked his corn, hauled it from the field and threw it into the corncrib. He had a good crop and the crib was full. He then nailed up the doors of the cabin and the corncrib, saddled a mule, and rode out over the Marial–Hell's Gate Canyon trail to Grants Pass.

On the first of the following March, Ike came home, feeling much worse, but hungry for wild hog and his own liquor. While relieving his mule of saddle and bridle, he noticed that the door of the corn crib had been broken open and that fully half of his corn was gone. There was a well-beaten trail leading to the timber back of the crib, and another leading down to the hog pen. There were seven big wild hogs in the pen, and they were fat, too, with more corn lying on the ground than they could eat; and hogs can eat lots of corn.

Looking for sign, he could find only huge bear tracks. The cabin had not been disturbed, so Ike decided to lay low and see what would develop. Just after sundown a huge brown bear walked leisurely down the trail from the timber to the

corncrib, gathered his arms full of corn, carried it to the hog pen, and threw it into the hogs. After making four trips between hog pen and corncrib, he walked over to the old plum tree, reached up into the forks, pulled down the remains of a half-eaten hog, and ate his evening meal.

The day after Ike returned home he discovered that one of the bear's hogs would make good pork, so he shot it, dragged it out with a rope, dressed it, and hung it in his smokehouse. Watching from the cabin window that evening, he saw the old bear throw his first load of corn into the pen, then look at the hogs for several minutes. After each load of corn he seemed to be counting his hogs, and Ike always claimed the bear scratched his head. Soon, however, he went to the plum tree where he finished eating the remains of the hog which had furnished his dinner the evening before.

That night about midnight Ike was awakened by hearing a hog squealing at the top of its voice. The moon was full and looking out his window he saw the bear come into the clearing carrying a big hog which he heaved into the pen. Following that, every time either Ike or the bear took a hog from the pen, the bear caught and threw in another.

Ike Jones and the Rattlesnakes

One morning, Ike Jones, father of Hathaway, killed 400 rattlesnakes before breakfast. Killed them with a club. Ike owned a yoke of oxen which he used in all-round ranch work at his mountain home. The oxen were quite gentle and seldom ranged far. When the day's work was done, Ike would just unyoke them and turn them loose.

Early one summer morning he discovered the oxen had wandered away from their usual feeding ground, so he started out to find them. After walking some distance, he came to a large mound of broken rock, near which there was a large rattlesnake all coiled up and full of fight.

Ike searched around until he found a stout club with which he killed the snake. But more rattlesnakes kept crawling out of the rocks, hissing and rattling, and Ike killed them as fast as they came. Well, the snakes kept coming, and Ike kept clubbing them until he had killed 400; but by that time his eyes became blind from the fumes given off by the snakes. There were more snakes coming too. He could hear them rattling, but not being able any longer to see them, he backed away, felt his way to a nearby creek, washed the venom vapor out of his eyes, and went home for breakfast.

Ike's Maple Shoe Pegs

Times were hard on the lower Rogue. The winter of '81 and '82 was long and very cold. "Skinners" had killed most of the deer, elk, and bear, taking the hides and leaving the meat to waste. There had been a little corn which the people had home ground; and there were a few domestic hogs. Cougars, bobcats, and the few remaining bears had preyed upon the wild hogs until only a few old savage boars were left, and they were not fit for food.

Predatory animals became so desperate from hunger they killed the cattle and horses except where they were close guarded; an Indian woman was killed and eaten by cougars. One morning just after daylight John Fry heard his last hog squealing "like grim death." Looking out of the window he saw, out in the barnyard, a huge bear sitting up on his haunches with the hog in his arms, head down. The bear was eating the hog alive, eating its hams, while all the hog could do was squeal in protest. So John shot the bear, and the hog too, and the family ate them both.

The spring of '82 was so wet no one could raise much garden; cutworms destroyed all the young corn plants, and potato bugs ruined the potato crop. Times were desperate indeed, and there all the people of the section gathered at the John Fry place for the purpose of evolving, if possible, a course of action which would save them from starvation. Several ideas were suggested, discussed, and discarded as impractical and hopeless. The situation appeared baffling; everyone was downcast and silent, and some were preparing to leave for their homes. Through all the meeting Ike Jones had been sitting to one side saying nothing, but he now arose and announced that he had a plan which would no doubt solve their problem.

In olden days, as everyone knows, shoe pegs were made of wood, and maple was considered best for that purpose. Ike called attention to the maple trees which were plentiful, and suggested everybody, old and young, get to work whittling out maple shoe pegs. If they all worked hard they would have a great number of shoe pegs by December 1st, and he would take them to San Francisco, sell them and return by Christmas with provisions purchased with the money they would bring. He assured them he was familiar with the coast trail, having traveled it the time he crossed the Oregon line thirty minutes ahead of the posse.

Returning to their homes, the folk all started whittling maple wood shoe pegs. John Fry was very clever with an ax, so he split wood for the whittlers. The pegs were well made, round, and sharp at one end. Even the small children became quite adept at whittling. And so they worked, whittling from daylight to dark, all summer and fall.

Beginning on the 15th of November, Ike Jones, who lived farthest upriver, started gathering up the shoe pegs and mules. His outfit had whittled enough for one mule load, or 300 pounds. Each family turned their pegs over to Ike, with enough mules for their transportation. Finally, at John Fry's place, after the last peg had been gathered, they had all that thirty mules could carry. Four of the mules were small, so they were only required to pack 250 pounds.

Bright and early on the morning of December 1st, 1882, Ike Jones, with two Indian helpers, pulled out for San Francisco with the mule train all packed with maple shoe pegs. They followed the old Indian trail along the ridge, down into Windy Valley and on to the Chetco which they forded above tidewater. From there they followed the old trail to Ukiah, Clear Lake, and Sacramento, and from there traveled to San Francisco by steamboat.

When, however, they tried to sell their wooden shoe pegs,

they discovered that iron shoe pegs had been invented, and that wooden pegs were no longer used. No one would buy their pegs. So Ike led the pack train out near the Mission, where he and his Indians relieved them of their packs and saddles and turned them out to grass. While they were making camp one mule kept nosing around the sacks of pegs and an Indian seeing it said: "Him likum oats," and right at that very moment Ike, whose mind was keen, thought of a fine commercial scheme.

He and both Indians, by whittling feverishly all night, succeeded by ten o'clock the next morning in sharpening the other ends of all the pegs. They then packed them on the mules, took them downtown to a big feed and grain store and sold them for oats.

With the money thus obtained they purchased all the provisions the thirty mules could carry, returned to the waterfront and caught the same steamboat to Sacramento. From there they cut straight across the wilds for home, as Ike considered it advisable to avoid the trails, and arrived at John Fry's place on the 24th of December. Everybody was there to welcome Ike, the news of his coming having preceded him via grapevine. One mule carried 300 pounds of candy for the children, and there were provisions in plenty for all, so they enjoyed a merry Christmas.

Ike Jones and the Great Rattler

Ike Jones spent a great deal of time trying to educate his boy, Hathaway, in the art of lying, and, while the young man showed promise, the old man thought his son was a little backward. Possibly had the old man lived long enough, he might have been proud of Hathaway. But Ike starved to death.

While prospecting in the mountains northeast of the Big Bend, Ike lived in a cabin which had one door and one small window. One day, about four miles from his cabin, he ran onto a terrible snake. It was fifteen feet long, thick as a man's leg, with a head as big as a pumpkin.

Right away he started running and the snake started rattling and striking. Ike ran fast with long strides, but for every stride, the snake would coil, rattle, and strike. Away they went, up the mountains and down the canyons, Ike stretching his legs with every stride, while the snake coiled, rattled, and struck, strike for strike.

At last Ike gained his cabin with the rattlesnake right behind him. Darting into the shack, he slammed the door, catching the snake's strike in full force. The door was three inches thick, but the snake struck it so hard he drove his fangs right through, so that an inch of each fang stuck out into the room.

Ike grabbed a hammer and clinched the ends of the fangs so the snake could not pull them out, but in so doing, he sealed his own doom. The old snake rattled and shook the cabin like

[3 4]

a varmint dog shaking a skunk, but the door held. In time, Ike ran out of grub, the window was so small he could not crawl through it, and the rattlesnake would not let him out the door. So Ike starved to death, just when he was ready to die of thirst.

Ike Jones's Woodpecker

One time while Ike Jones was walking through the woods, he came upon an old dead tree which had fallen through the night. There had been a woodpecker's nest in the tree, but it was destroyed by the fall, and all but one of the baby woodpeckers was dead.

Now Ike was a softhearted man, besides he felt lonesome. So he carried the little woodpecker to his cabin and fed him some flies. There were plenty around Ike's cabin. The little fellow seemed to like flies, but Ike went out and broke up an old log from which he recovered a quantity of termites, grubs, and bugs of various sorts. These he spread out before the young woodpecker. The little fellow looked them over carefully, then ate the biggest one; whereupon Ike named him Solomon III, he claiming to be Solomon II.

Solomon III grew fast. Soon he was able to hustle food for himself, but he always liked to have Ike break up logs for him. He became as large as a small hen, but had a head as red as a rose, and a bill that was long and sharp. "He understood everything said to him, and he was as smart as a man, smarter than some," added Hathaway.

Solomon III and Ike were always together. They carried on long conversations during which Ike would put Solomon's opinions into words. They sang old hymns together, making sounds which were outlandishly weird.

One spring Ike took the planting fever and raised a patch of corn. It grew so tall it looked like trees, and the ears, four or five to the stalk, were so high Ike could only reach a few of them. He talked the matter over with Solomon III and, after much discussion, formulated a plan of action.

Ike built a big corncrib on the hill near the corn patch. Solomon watched the building with great interest, and, when it was finished, flew under the eaves and began pecking a hole. So Ike fetched his auger and bored a hole. He then took an ear of corn, shelled a handful and poured it through the hole, explaining to Solomon while so doing that all the corn had to be put through that hole.

Next day Solomon worked hard all day, back and forth from the corn fields to the corncrib, but one woodpecker could not make very much impression upon so large a job, so Ike told him he better get some help.

Next morning after breakfast Solomon flew away to engage extra hands. All day long woodpeckers began arriving, and when Solomon came home with 10,000, there were at least 100,000 woodpeckers on the job. They all worked with a will, and by noon of the third day, all the corn was harvested, shelled, and in the corncrib.

When the job was done a great dispute arose between Solomon III and several leaders of the woodpecker laborers, but Solomon began singing "This World is not My Home," and it was not long before Ike and Solomon were alone.

The following winter Ike set up his still and he and Solomon spent the long winter evenings in scandalous wassail. However, when spring came, Solomon III took up with a little redhead, flew away, and never returned.

Ike Jones and Lucifer

Ike Jones, after his wife died and his children had all drifted away on their own, lived close to nature. And while he depended upon hunting and trapping for sustenance, he never harmed any creature except for food or fur. He loved all birds, and each morning scattered food for the quail. They were mountain quail, as that is the only kind native to the Rogue River district, and they are the largest and most beautiful of all the quail family.

They became used to Ike and quite tame. Sometimes when there was snow and Ike would be late a-rising, hundreds of the pert little fellows would collect around his cabin, calling and scolding, while waiting for their breakfast. When on such occasions he opened his door, they would crowd into the cabin and light on him so thick he could hardly move.

They were always in the cabin whenever they could get in, and at mealtimes would sit around waiting for crumbs. Should a stranger approach the cabin, they would either flush in a cloud with a roar of wings, or else streak away into the brush, but as soon as the visitor departed, out they would come from every direction.

Now of all predatory animals, the bobcat is the most fond of quail, but Ike's quail enjoyed perfect protection from that menace. Ike had a pet bobcat. He found him in a den when he was just a little fellow, and took him home to his cabin. The kitten was hard to gentle, and Ike suffered many scratches and bites before the young varmint became peaceful. Ike's kindness, however, and his care, eventually reached the cat's heart, and then he became gentle in the extreme.

Ike named his bobcat Lucifer on account of the way he acted when small. He grew up to weigh 80 pounds. Lucifer always had an eye open for dogs, and knew just how to whip them. Springing upon them with the fury of a demon, crushing them with his weight, and scratching and biting, even the toughest old hounds would just go yelping down the trail, with no stomach for fight.

Lucifer was trained from kittenhood to accept quail as part of the family. He not only seemed to love them, he made it his business to protect them. Sleeping in the sunshine before the cabin door, the quail would run all over him, but he did not mind. While he was eating they would gather around and peck at his food, sitting on him, and making themselves at home, but he never scolded them.

He seemed to always know whenever any wild bobcat ranged near his home. On such occasions he would slink away into the woods, and then it would not be long before sounds of a super cat fight would resound through the forest. Then, after a short time, Lucifer would come into the cabin and

crawl under the blankets with Ike. They always slept together. Some of the wild ones he fought were tough old toms,
but he was quite able to handle them. He was fighting for
principle. He had hundreds of quail dependents to protect
and, fired with that humane or bobcat incentive, he was in-
vincible.

One spring a family settled down the canyon from Ike's
place. They had one child, a little girl about two years old.
She, Ike, and Lucifer became great friends. She was the only
human being other than Ike who ever won the affections of
that big cat. He became very much attached to the little girl,
and frequently carried rabbits and gray squirrels to her.

The child, while playing one evening near the edge of the
woods a short distance from the cabin, was seized by a cougar
and carried away. Hearing her screams, her parents ran after
her, the father carrying his rifle. By the cougar's tracks, and
bits of clothing clinging to the brush, they were able to find
the way easily.

Down the trail they plodded, that mother and father, sick
at heart, full of despair and utterly hopeless, their tears falling
upon the indifferent earth. Soon they came to a small open
space in the woods, and there they saw their little girl pleading
with the bobcat, Lucifer, to "wake up," but he was quite dead.
And off to one side there was a large female cougar also dead.

The signs were plain for any woodsman to read. Lucifer
had been carrying a rabbit; it was there on the ground, no
doubt fetching it to the child. He had met the cougar carrying
the little girl to her den for her kittens. A furious fight ensued
and Lucifer killed the cougar, but in so doing he laid down
his own life for his little friend.

The father took off his coat and spread it gently over the body of the bobcat. Next day that little family and old Ike Jones buried Lucifer and marked his grave with a headboard which, after these many years, has not disappeared.

Ike's Raven, "Lemuel"

Old Ike Jones was a veteran of the Mexican War, Kentucky Volunteers. He liked Mexico, and after the war, returned and lived there for several years, expecting to make that his permanent home. Unfortunately he made love to the wrong girl and decided to hurry to points north of the border.

During his long life he always had pet birds, animals, and even reptiles. His pet toad smoked cigarettes. While in Mexico he was taught by an old Indian parrot peddler how to so operate upon the tongues of birds they were enabled to pronounce words. He taught a magpie to repeat many things, but it never originated anything.

His raven, however, could think and carry on a conversation. Ike had some heated arguments with the bird over politics. Of course Ike was a Democrat, while the raven was a black Republican. Like many of his pets, Ike raised the raven from the time it was quite young, having stolen it from the nest where it was hatched.

The operation upon its tongue was very successful. It soon discovered it could talk, and always seemed anxious to learn, especially profanity, of which Ike possessed a remarkable vocabulary, both English and Spanish.

Ike named his raven Lemuel, after the prophet, because the bird liked to eat corn that had been soaked overnight in moonshine. Whenever Lemuel wanted some of that stimulating delicacy he would inform Ike of his craving by such statements as: "Give strong drink unto him that is about to perish! Hell, Ike, it's your treat."

Lemuel was a great help in hunting. Riding on Ike's shoulder, he would go out into the woods with Ike until they came to some place where there might be deer, then Lemuel would fly all around looking. Spotting a deer, he would croak like ordinary wild ravens, except he croaked three times, then paused, then repeated. Hearing the signal, Ike knew just where to find the deer.

A big old plum tree grew near the cabin. When ripe the plums were large, yellow, and luscious. Lemuel thought the plums were very fine; so did the wild ravens. Lemuel figured out a plan of strategy which was quite effective as a means of protecting the fruit. Early in the morning he would hide in the plum tree and wait for the wild ones. Sooner or later several would circle around then make for the tree, there to be met with a stream of profanity that sounded just like Ike. Away they would fly with Lemuel right after them calling them awful names. It was a common sight to see a flock of ravens flying as fast as they could, pursued by Lemuel whooping and cussing so loud he could be heard a mile.

Ike and Lemuel were once hunting several miles from the

cabin in a rough canyon where a boulder upon which Ike was standing gave away causing him to fall, and the boulder rolled upon his foot. He soon discovered he would need help if he were ever to extricate himself. It was a long way to the nearest neighbor. Regardless of help he was going to stay where he was all night, for the sun had already set.

Making himself as comfortable as possible, Ike told Lemuel to go get him something to eat. The raven flew away, soon returning with a big piece of jerky. The next trip he brought a piece of bread, and the third trip he carried a half pint bottle of moonshine. Ike then told Lemuel to go get Johnnie Fry and have him bring an ax.

John Fry's place was thirty miles away, air line, and Lemuel arrived there just before dark. John was in the house eating supper when he heard some one calling: "Johnnie, bring an ax." He opened the door and there stood Ike Jones's raven. After greeting him with "Howdy, Lemuel," John asked him what he wanted, and even now, when John is very old and always speaks the truth, he says the raven told him Ike had his foot caught under a rock and needed help with an ax.

So John saddled a horse, picked up an ax, and set out up the river trail, with Lemuel riding on his shoulder. They hurried along, talking about this and that, to within half a mile of their destination, left the horse and walked to where Ike was being held by the boulder. John cut a small fir and fashioned a lever with which he pried up the rock far enough for Ike to pull out his foot. After helping Ike to the horse, they all went down to the cabin where Lemuel received a generous portion of bread soaked in moonshine. Johnnie and Ike drank theirs straight.

Ike Jones Calls the Hogs

There came a time when winter was closing in upon the Rogue country. Ike, sitting in the door of his cabin trying to absorb the last bit of warmth from the wintry sun which was setting behind the blue western mountains, felt old and lonely. He was old, too, very old. No longer could he roam the forests and mountains, carrying home his game; nor could he ever again trap fisher and martin along the high ridges when the snow was deep and wintry gales howled through the canyons and wailed across the barren crags and peaks.

He felt the chill of coming night. It was getting cold. Reading the signs of nature he knew the winter ahead would be long and hard. His supplies were meager, and he would have no furs with which to purchase more. He was just a poor, old, lonely man burdened with the weight of years.

When a mere boy, he had left his native hills in faraway Kentucky, and always he had fared along through the summer heat and winter cold, liking most of all to brave the storms of snow that other men had to face and sleet and the wind which scattered treetops and broken limbs like feathers. Now, all that was left was a little old man who must sit by his stove and dream of the past, fearing for the first time in all his venturesome life he might be hungry.

Now all the time Ike was thus commiserating with himself, his pet sow, Jezebel, kept rooting him gently and rubbing her side against his leg. Jezebel was a privileged character around Ike's place. He had raised her from pighood, and he claimed she was more dependable than people. He often confided to his few visitors that Jezebel never acted like human beings. She was always just a hog, while human beings were not always human. They sometimes acted like hogs.

Jezebel was so persistent in grunting and rubbing against Ike's leg that he finally comprehended what she was trying to convey. She was telling him, in the only way she could, that the side of a hog makes good bacon, and that bacon would keep during the winter. The woods were full of wild hogs. They were fat too, because the acorn and myrtle nut crops were exceptionally heavy that year. Thinking it over, he knew he could shoot plenty hogs, but he could not carry them home.

Dwelling on the problem, his mind drifted back to the days of his childhood. He remembered how his father, at hog-killing time, climbed onto the housetop and called the razorbacks in from all the surrounding hills. He decided to try the old hog call out on Jezebel, and if it worked with her he would try it on the wild hogs. So he gave the call, kind of low and gentle, and Jezebel, from the back yard where she had wandered, came waddling to him as fast as her condition would permit, and stood before him inquiringly. Ike asked her how she would like to be made into bacon, ham, and lard. She replied with a grunt, walked into the cabin, and laid down back of the stove to get warm. While Ike, satisfied now that the call would work, went in by the stove also. So engrossed was he in his plans of calling hogs and smoking bacon he failed to notice, until his teeth began to chatter, that he had forgotten to build a fire.

It was very cold that night. The following morning the

ground was frozen and white with frost. Good hog-killing weather, Ike reflected. So, after breakfast, and after Jezebel, there being no dog, had finished cleaning the dishes and the frying pan, old Ike clambered up a ladder to the roof of his cabin, taking his rifle with him. Inhaling a long breath he began calling. The more he called the stronger his voice became until the echoes rolled back and forth across the canyon, and the hogs began to arrive. First, a lone hog, then two, then several, then whole herds came. Big old boars with tusks curled up a foot over their snouts, their high shoulders covered with bristles six inches long; sows with pigs clinging to their tits and squealing for their breakfast; black hogs, red hogs, white hogs, spotted hogs, all shapes, sizes, and colors.

By ten o'clock Ike estimated a 1,000 hogs and 500 pigs were gathered around his cabin, all looking up at him with steadfast gaze. Long since Ike had stopped calling, but hogs continued to arrive. By midafternoon there were so many the cabin-clearing could not hold them and the surrounding woods were crowded. Ike was sure 10,000 hogs, not including thousands of pigs, had come at his bidding, all of them standing around in answer to the Old Kentucky Hog Call.

Most of the hogs were in good order. Ike, figuring he could eat a lot of bacon and hams through the winter, decided to shoot fifty of the best. Taking careful aim at the head of a fine fat shoat, he was pressing the trigger when a thought came that caused him to lower his rifle. Ike felt foolish. He suddenly recalled that he had never got around to building his big smokehouse. There was no place to smoke his hams and bacon.

[47]

Misadventures of Ike Jones

Ike Jones, like most old people, was absent-minded. With him that mental state was not merely intermittent, it was a fixed idiosyncrasy that frequently caused him discomfort, but he always treated the weakness and himself with good-natured tolerance. One time he had been fishing in the Rogue, and having caught a forty-pound Chinook salmon, started carrying it to his cabin which was not more than one fourth mile distant. While walking along he became interested in his plans of the smokehouse he intended building before winter. So absorbed was he in the subject, that he passed right by his cabin and went on up the mountain trail for three miles. He was so tired he had to lay down the salmon and rest. He often told about that experience as a good joke on himself.

Another time he arranged with an Indian, who owned a boat, to take him downriver to Gold Beach for a load of supplies. Upon arriving at that town he purchased his goods and had the merchant place them in a pile in one corner of the store. He then proceeded to visit around town where he enjoyed talking with old friends. On the morning of the fifth day, becoming tired of town, he and his Indian started homeward at daylight.

That was before motors were used in Rogue River boats. Navigation on the river was accomplished by rowing, poling, and towing by hand. Ike and the Indian worked hard all day. Toward evening they landed at a bar eighteen miles up the river where they stopped to cook their supper and camp for the night. Telling the Indian to build a fire, Ike stepped down to the boat for some provisions when he suddenly remembered his supplies. They were still in a pile in a corner of the store at Gold Beach.

The Two-Headed Snake

"Ike was the damnedest feller for pets I ever did see," said Hatfield, "birds, annimules, crawlin' critters, most everything but fleas, and he tried hard to civilize some of them, but he kept losing his cozen fleas among the crowd."

"I droppen in for a set," he continued, "and a couple of drinks with Ike. We had two or three, maybe more, when Ike up and says I look like I was drunk. Said he never seed me drunk before, so now he supposed I was headed for the dogs and a drunken grave. Course, I was cold sober, considering the company I was keepin', and I just laughed at him. Then he pinted at the floor and says, 'How many snakes do you see?' 'Two,' says I. 'Ye're drunk,' says Ike, 'they's only one snake.' 'Go outside,' he says to the snake, and out it crawled. Then I see one snake crawling and decided maybe I better taper off, but soon as Ike had his fun with me he called the snake back in and showed me it was one critter with two heads. Believe me, I had Ike's jug ringin' holler 'fore I left a couple days later."

The Wild Hog Derby

Fourth of July celebration was in full swing at Dogwood Park on the old home ranch of John and Ike Fry; the year was 1884. Dancing on the outdoor floor continued day and night without intermission. There were plenty fiddlers and harmonica players, so when one set became tired, another would take its place, and the woman who played the organ seemed to never grow tired. The dancing crowd merely took time out for snacks and cat naps.

There was never a time when there were not at least half a dozen babies squalling. Those were the days of large families, and the park was alive with small boys who climbed all the trees and girls with starched dresses and pigtails. They had boy races, girl races, and boy and girl races, the latter being won by a long-legged girl from Ellensburg who, years later, taught school at Potato Illahe.

The barbecue pits were kept going, and during the celebration they would dispose of six steers, numerous sheep, and as many bucks as were brought in. Everyone brought food of some kind, and there was enough and more for all. There was moonshine for those who wished it and soda pop for the children. The soda pop was packed in from Grants Pass, one hundred miles over the mountains. All the people of the lower Rogue came to the celebration. Ranchers, miners, prospectors, breeds, whites, and Indians gathered together in the name of liberty.

The older folk sat around on benches or the ground and visited. Local domestic problems were discussed and, of course, among the women there was a little gossip. And so, during the drifting trend of the conversation, someone remarked that they had raced most everything but wild animals. The burro race had furnished the most excitement and amusement, next to the fat woman's race. Whereupon they indulged in considerable speculation concerning the speed of different animals.

Ike Jones said he had an old sow that could outrun and outfight any hound dog in the country. John Fry offered to bet his best varmint dog against the sow that the dog could catch and throw her, but Ike already had too many dogs. Everybody always had too many hound dogs. Still, Ike agreed they might make the bet, but it would have to be decided several weeks later, on account of the sow's maternal prospects. Then they started talking about wild hogs.

Ike claimed that wild hogs were smarter than most people, and not much different in their instincts. And, he thought they were so intelligent they could, with a little training, be developed into right good race hogs. This brought on numerous stories of the wild ones, and the day passed, as old Johnnie remembers it, in swapping lies about wild boars, their habits and general dispositions.

[51]

The following afternoon while a number of men were sitting on a long bench resting after a game of horseshoes, and, after visiting Ike Jones's tent for a "snort of moon," wild hogs once again became the topic of conversation. It was started by a bright remark from John Fry. While at Grants Pass after the soda pop, he had obtained a copy of the *Police Gazette* which contained the story of a horse race held in England called the derby and, being intrigued by the name, announced to all within hearing that: "Next year we are going to hold a Wild Hog Derby."

Old John Billings wanted to know: "How in the Hell they could put hats on wild hogs," but allowed a derby hat might look all right on an old wild boar. Everyone had something to say about derby hats on hogs, except Frank Fry, proud owner of the only derby hat on the lower Rogue. He told them in no uncertain terms that his hat was not going to be worn by any hog. Finally John told them about the English Derby which, he explained, was a horse race for three year olds; but, he then added, that if they raced wild hogs they would race porkers of any age, because on Fourth of July they should rebel against the British in everything.

The whole subject would no doubt have been worn out and dropped had not Ike Jones insisted they could catch old wild hogs and teach them to race. He admitted the rules would have to be liberal, seeing that hogs are set in their ways and no amount of education could develop them into anything but hogs. While racing, they would be permitted to crowd and fight because they would do so regardless of rules.

They talked over all the difficulties which would have to

be overcome (there were plenty of them) and tried to solve the many problems incident to such an event. It was not clear just how they could get the wild hogs, but all agreed they would have to be "big old wild ones." Ike Jones volunteered to furnish all the hogs for the event, but they turned that down, agreeing with Antone Walker, the Portuguese, that every man should catch and train his own race hog. Ike flared up and wanted to know if they thought he might cheat, and everybody cried in chorus: "We know darn well you would!"

The rest of the day was passed with much banter and laughter at each other's expense, Frank Fry and his derby being ridden the hardest. They decided to hold the Wild Hog Derby during the Fourth of July celebration the following year, and perfected all plans. A place for the track was selected and a date set when all were to come and help fence it. It was to be ten feet wide and one quarter mile long. Each owner would be allowed, when the race was on, to call his hog. The spectators could do as they pleased, but they would be requested to refrain from throwing rocks at the racers, or bothering them with sticks. Either boars or sows could be entered and all comers were welcome.

Now at that time all the lower Rogue country was fine hog pasture, and besides thousands of wild ones, everybody had domestic hogs. They earmarked their pigs and usually managed to have plenty pork. Some families scalded and scraped the hair off hogs, but most of them just skinned them like deer or bear. There were no fences and with fine range, it was natural for some hogs to prefer the wild state. Eventually many of the third or fourth and following generations developed the looks and habits of regular wild hogs with high shoulders, long snouts, and great tusks. Some of the boars grew to huge proportions.

Those who knew agreed they would rather fight a she-bear with cubs than an old wild sow with pigs because the sow would call in the whole herd and they were gang fighters. If an unarmed person met a wild boar, he had to climb a tree or run for his life. Running was a sure way of escape, as wild boars have to do a lot of backing and starting, while they chomp their teeth, slobber, snap at imaginary things in the air, working themselves into a rage. Then, after getting all ready to charge, and discovering the man can no longer be seen, they work off their anger by slashing trees, bushes, or anything which is handy.

A good portion of the time during the last days of the 1884 Fourth of July celebration was devoted to talk concerning the coming wild hog race. Everybody had some plan for catching them, although the plans were always for someone besides themselves.

Johnnie Fry determined to catch his wild one in his log "bear pen" down in Copper Canyon, and eventually he did catch a huge auburn-colored boar with long sharp tusks. He almost depleted the early cabbage patch for bait and caught any number of the wrong kind of hogs before his big fellow, allowing his appetite to overcome the sense of caution which experience had developed through contact with human beings, walked into the pen and sprung the trap.

The brute was old, mean, and red-eyed with anger. Looking through the logs at what he had caught, John felt like running away, or climbing a tree. The boar was "raring up" and slashing the logs with his tusks, backing across the pen until his rear end banged against the wall, biting the air as though he could see things floating around, and maybe he could. No one knows what mad hogs can see.

John caught his wild boar during the dreamy days of late summer, and left him in the bear pen until the rainy season set in, then moved him to a strong pen down back of the barn. During all this time the old fellow remained unfriendly, raging and slobbering at the mere sight of John, but at heart he was just a hog, so he ate his food and rooted around for more. But John built a roof over the pen and piled hay in one corner and, with cold weather, the boar grew fat and more gentle.

"Portugee Tony Walker" spread the news that he had a big black boar with lines like a thoroughbred race horse. Indian Ned had captured a boar with a black body and a white head from which one ear had been bitten off by some predatory animal. The breeds were all backing Indian Ned's hog with whatever they had to wager, which was very little.

Old John Billings duly entered his hog, a black boar with red spots and tusks ten inches long. He was the ruling, vicious, cantankerous leader of a great herd that ranged from Illahe to High Ridge, battle scarred from fights with bears, cougars, and other boars. Billings caught him in a pitfall.

The old boar was brave, but experienced and cautious, knowing that men are dangerous. Old Billings, however, knew all about hogs, and he knew where the herd was "using" in a big myrtle bottom where the ground was covered with nuts. Selecting a main runway, he dug a pit, covered it with sticks, and laid leaves and trash over the top. He had a very smart dog that was with him while he prepared the pit.

[55]

The next day old John saw the boar coming along the runway near the pit. Undisturbed, the boar would walk around the pit, but John "sicked" his dog at him. The dog was small, so the impatient old hog charged; the dog ran and jumped over the pit, while the boar plunged into it. It required some contriving before they were able to get the old boar out of the pit. They first succeeded in getting him to fight a quantity of gill net until he became all tangled up and unable to hardly move, then they hoisted him up with blocks and tackle rigged from the limb of a myrtle tree, lowered him onto a sled to which a team of horses was hitched, hauled him home, and put him into a stout pen.

Of course Ike Jones had a race hog. He refused to talk about it, and no one could discover anything, either, because there were always wild hogs around his place. But a couple of weeks before the Fourth of July celebration for 1885 was scheduled to start, he walked into Dogwood Park leading a long-legged, long-bodied, slab-sided, old, wild, windsplitter sow, with ears that flopped down like those of a hound dog. She was brick red, and had a ring in her nose from which led a stout cord. She followed Ike just like a horse or a dog.

The track was cleared and fenced and at the starting end a large pen was constructed and partitioned into five compartments for each of which there was a chute running to the track. Built in at the pen end of each chute a door was contrived which could be raised, permitting the racer clear egress to the track.

Each day the race hogs were trained and exercised by the owners, but only one hog was allowed on the track at any time. At exercise time the owner of a hog would be turned into the track, and after it traversed the quarter mile, it received its meal. They soon learned to go for their feed, but getting them back to the pen was quite another thing. However, the Jones sow just trotted down to her dinner and permitted herself to be led back peacefully.

Antone Walker entered a protest claiming that Ike Jones was running a tame hog. At the hearing Ike dared Tony to get into the pen with his sow. He climbed in and the sow attacked him with a fury that caused him to climb out and withdraw his protest.

Betting became an obsession. Everything was wagered upon some hog and right on his nose too. Some bet on one race hog against the field, while others made bets respecting two particular hogs. With these speculators it made no difference which hog won the race.

"Portugee Tony Walker's" black boar was the favorite because he covered the quarter in practice faster than any of the others. Going down the track he paced, while the others all trotted. No hog will ever lope or run unless greatly frightened, and these hogs were not afraid of anything except guns.

The hogs were not fed on the day of the race and by two o'clock in the afternoon they were hungry and ill-tempered. They acted as though they hated the sight of each other, except Ike Jones's sow; she was indifferent. A stranger was picked for starter and promptly at two o'clock the gates were raised and he fired a shot into the air. He then emptied his gun for good measure and every race hog fairly shot out through the chutes onto the track. Here they crowded and pitched into a fight, something they had craved to do since first seeing each other. But a small boy touched off a bunch of firecrackers and threw it among them, greatly to their consternation. They had, each in his time, been shot at, and so they ran for their lives, with Ike Jones's red sow in the lead.

They were running fine until the John Billings boar side-swiped the Portuguese hog, cutting a gash in his shoulder and causing him to squeal. The red sow, now far in the lead, heard the squeal and, hog-like, turned and trotted back. Whenever a hog squeals, all the others run to him, bristles up and ready for trouble.

Instantly the race once more turned into a free-for-all fight, and Indian Ned's boar was so severely tusked he laid down and died. Another bunch of firecrackers was thrown in, but it fell on the wrong side of the fight, stampeding the four remaining racers back toward the starting end of the track. Seeing this, the starter turned loose with his six-shooter and sent them back.

During all this time the owners were calling, but the only hog that seemed to hear was Ike's sow, and with all the fighting and squealing she became confused. Coming to Indian Ned's dead hog they all stopped to inspect him, and right away the three remaining boars plunged into battle. John Billing's old herd leader hurt Portuguese Tony's boar with a mortal stab of his tusk, and he started walking away. Ike's sow heard her master calling and trotted toward the finish line. She would have won the race, too, but someone who had bet against her started shooting into the air and turned her back. In the meantime, the Portuguese, feeling very sick, and bleeding profusely, walked slowly across the line, winner of the Wild Hog Derby.

After the Billings and John Fry boars had cut each other to pieces and laid down and died, Ike called his sow across

the line and was given second money. The Portuguese walked about twenty feet after winning the race and died from loss of blood.

So ended the Wild Hog Derby on the lower Rogue. Now, the dogwood trees in the old park bloom just the same in the springtime, but the round corral has long since fallen down. Where the dance hall stood during the old days there are now just some pieces of broken board. The benches are all gone, and of all those old-timers who sat upon them, John Fry alone remains. It has been many years since the Fourth of July was celebrated at Dogwood Park; the fiddles and the harmonicas are heard no more, but in the evening, there are thrushes and the robins.

The Adventures of Sampson Jones

The Birth and Childhood of Sampson Jones

Ike Jones and his wife made arrangements with an old Indian woman who was often engaged to help babies into the world. In her naïve mannerism this old squaw occasionally observed that she could not understand why anyone would want to come hither; and that, evidently, considering the way babies cried and made faces, they were never at all pleased with the impressions gained from their first glimpses of this "vale of tears," or "howling wilderness," as the case may be. She and Mrs. Ike Jones calculated, by means of those homely but wise "deductions" known to all women, the approximate date when, in the orderly course of nature, the time of her delivery would come upon her; and the squaw midwife agreed to be at the Jones's cabin in advance of the "stork."

When the time arrived for the old squaw to begin her walk of thirty miles over the mountain trails, it was midwinter and raining in a manner known to few places other than the lower Rogue country. But she made a bundle of her various necessaries, including a supply of dried wormwood, it being the season when green wormwood could not be found, and with utter indifference respecting the weather began her journey. However, toward evening, a wild steer gored and trampled her to death, and her mangled body was devoured by bears, wolves, and other predatory animals.

A few nights later the mother-to-be was taken with pains.

She had been ill for some time and was very weak. Ike helped her all he could, and, during the small hours of the morning, a baby boy was born. But the mother, not being able to survive the ordeal, passed away within the hour of her son's birth.

During the night the storm had attained dreadful fury. Rain came down in sheets, driven by a gale that howled and screamed around the cabin. Great trees were crashing down all around, blinding flashes of lightning were almost constant, while thunder roared and rumbled and echoed across the mountains. Neighbors were few and far away, and Ike had nothing wherewith to feed the baby. Stunned and full of grief over his wife's death, utterly alone and bewildered, he cuddled his little son in a blanket and sat by the fire, wrapt in total desolation.

Hardships, going without and contriving to get along— all those things were part of life with Ike, but now the familiar fortitude which had carried him through many dangers seemed to have died within him; he felt lost, broken and hopeless. He had always considered death to be merely a part of life, and in its presence had never before been perturbed. Now, sitting there alone, helpless while his child lay in his arms starving, it seemed more than he could bear.

Now it happened that during the spring three years previous to the birth of Ike Jones's son he had found, while hunting, the den of a cougar family. Without the slightest compunction he had shot both of the parent cougars, but, having done that, he began worrying about their kittens, provided there were any. After considerable argument with himself he climbed up to the den and there, curled up together in a nest were two little spotted fellows that instantly appealed to the heart of Ike Jones.

He carried them home and just so that his wife would raise no objections gave them to her. He told her how hard he had worked getting them for her because she had been wanting a cat. So, like all good wives she pretended she believed him, and seeing the kittens were so cute, fell in love with them herself.

They had quite a time raising the young cougars. The male lived only a few days because he would not eat, but the female thrived. She would drink soup, eat boiled potatoes, and loved fried pork. They never gave her anything but cooked food. She had her bed in the woodshed which was built onto the cabin, but while she was small she slept with the folk. When she grew too large for that they experienced a lot of trouble breaking her. Finally, however, they discovered she would be contented in the woodshed provided they put her to bed and covered her with a blanket. Ike wanted to give the cougar some Biblical name, but his wife, being of a more modern turn of mind, finally convinced him that he wanted her named Toots.

If the wise scientists who claim the cat family to be devoid of affection could have known Toots, they would have admitted that there are exceptions. She was always underfoot, and she absolutely refused to be insulted. She never knew what it was to be hurt, because Ike and his wife were kindly folk.

One time after several days of restlessness Toots disap-

peared. Mrs. Ike was getting ready to cry about that, but chose rather to smile in a knowing way after Ike explained that Toots was likely having a love affair. So, about a week before Mrs. Jones was confined, Toots gave birth to a pair of little spotted kittens of whom she was very proud. Two or three times each day she carried the kittens to the bed where Mrs. Ike spent a great portion of her time, and while they were being petted would sit and purr so loud she sounded like a sawmill.

Gray dawn was beginning to show through the window, the baby was crying weakly, and unheeded tears were dripping down over the stern and rugged face of Ike Jones, when the mother cougar came from where she had been standing by the dead woman's bed, and laid her head upon his knee. Reaching up with her great paw, she patted the bundle in Ike's arms; patted it so gently her touch was light and soft as down. She then laid down on the floor and commenced making the sounds she used when calling her kittens to nurse. When Ike paid her no heed, she reached up a paw and pulled none too gently at his knee. So Ike helped the baby while it nursed the cougar.

Ike named his boy Sampson because he had long hair when he was born. Toots adopted the baby and he thrived. He was about a month old when John Fry, returning home over the mountains from Grants Pass, stopped in to visit and spend the night. He was the first human being Ike had seen since the birth of his child and the death of his wife, so he seized the opportunity to obtain a milk cow which John brought him within a few days.

Sampson did not care for cow's milk. He would drink it, but was not satisfied to go without cougar milk too. Also the only place he would sleep was curled up with the cougar. He made sounds like the kittens, and by the time Toots weaned him he could talk to her. Ike traded the two kittens to John Fry for the cow.

Sampson and Toots were together constantly, and after Sampson was four or five years old, they would lie on the floor for hours, both purring; then the boy would tell Ike weird and fantastic tales which he claimed the cougar had told him. He said Toots could close her eyes and see another world.

The Flat World of Sampson Jones

Sampson Jones, during the early days, lived on the Rogue at Battle Bar, just above Mule Creek. He said the world was flat, and he proved it. There was a big stump in front of his cabin upon which, after arguing upon the subject all afternoon with a prospector who claimed the world was not only round but that it turned around, he placed some rocks, holding that they would certainly fall off should the world turn upside down. The following morning the rocks were still upon the stump, and so far as Sampson Jones was concerned that settled the matter. "The world is flat," he said.

Sampson's Deer Jerky

Sampson Jones was a miner, but like many other men of that walk of life, found it necessary to pursue collateral activities at times when colors were few. Oregon had enacted a law which limited the killing of deer to certain months of late summer and fall, but Sampson did not subscribe to that legislation at all.

One day during the month of June he appeared at Gold Beach with three mules, each heavily packed with dried venison, known as "jerky," and proceeded to peddle it along the street to all who cared to buy. So they arrested him.

They hauled Sampson before the Justice of the Peace, rounded up a jury of twelve men, and tried him. Upon the jury were seven men who answered to the name Jones, because in Curry County, long ago, Jones was the name, just as Smith was the name in some other places. All members of the jury were miner-beachcombers.

Now Sampson Jones had friends. One man was sworn, took the stand, ate some of the dried meat, and solemnly pronounced it dried sturgeon. He swore he had dried thousands of pounds of sturgeon, and no one could fool him. Another just as positively identified the meat as mutton; another as calf; another as shark; another as goat; and another as mule, or possibly burro. In the meantime the jurors were all busily eating jerky.

The young lawyer who was District Attorney made a fine speech to the jerky-eating jury, chewing a little jerky himself between bursts of eloquence, and the case was submitted. The jury deliberated as long as any of them could eat jerky, filled all their pockets with evidence, and announced they had reached a verdict.

It read thus: "We the jury find the defendant not guilty, but recommend that he do not bring in so much at one load."

The Adventures of Hathaway Jones

The Big Potato Crop

On the lower Rogue, Hathaway Jones raised the heaviest crop of potatoes ever produced in the world. Up the river beyond Illahe, Jones squatted in an abandoned miner's cabin spending the winter trapping and sitting around. When spring came, he decided to go salmon fishing at Gold Beach, where Mr. Hume operated a cannery, and though his supplies were about exhausted, he still had more potatoes than he could use.

Noticing the steep hillside back of the cabin appeared to be good land, and there being no brush to clear away, he prepared quite a space with his shovel and planted his leftover potatoes.

He fished all summer, but returned to his cabin late in the fall, bringing with him three pack horse loads of supplies which he carried on his back. At Gold Beach, after he had loaded up, it occurred to him that with his pack on his back, his hands would be idle. So he picked up a couple of fifty-pound sacks of flour, and, by clasping his hands, easily carried a sack under each arm.

It was forty miles to his cabin up the river, but Hathaway made it in one day, walking his usual gait, arriving at his destination just at sunset. He said he lost three or four minutes time when he stopped to eat his lunch, because he was forced to lay down the two sacks of flour in order to free his hands.

One morning shortly after his return, while resting from carrying home a large fat bear and a five-point buck, one on each shoulder, from where he had killed them, back in the high mountains about six miles, he happened to think of the potatoes he had planted the previous spring. Picking up a shovel, he walked out and drove it with his foot deep under a hill and heaved it out. Then out of the hole he had made great big potatoes came rolling so fast, more than twelve bushels rolled out before he was able to plug the hole.

Sitting in his cabin by the fire during the long stormy season, Jones decided he would try some potatoes on bottom land where they could not roll on him, seeing those on the steep hillside almost buried him under an avalanche of spuds. So he went to work one morning, and by evening had cleared an acre of large myrtle trees. He dug up the trees and dragged them away by hand, because even the largest trees were only about three feet in diameter.

Later, after the April sun had warmed the soil, he planted the whole acre, putting a ten-pound potato in each hill, and covering them with a yard of rich loam. That accomplished, he once again repaired to the beach, where, among other things, he caught a salmon that weighed three hundred pounds, but turned it loose for fear the other fishermen seeing it might become discouraged.

The following fall, when ready to return home, and after he had his usual pack in place, he asked Bullhide Moore, the storekeeper, to throw a hundred-pound sack of potatoes on top of the load, because he entertained some doubt respecting the adaptability of myrtle bottom for gardening purposes.

The following morning, after a good night's rest, he decided to investigate his potato patch, so he started digging with his shovel. He found so many potatoes, and they were so big and long, there was not enough room upon which to pile them. He corded them up in ricks like stovewood, only higher, but was still short of room. At last he was compelled to clear another half acre of land upon which to pile potatoes. When he finished digging, he had a solid layer of potatoes seven feet high which completely covered an acre and one half of land; and in the whole lot not one potato weighed less than ten pounds.

Hathaway's Melons

During the early days watermelons were seldom seen on the lower Rogue. It was impossible to transport them over the roads, which were terrible, or over the trails, which were worse. Bouncing, jiggling, and bumping were always reducing the insides of melons to a mess. Small boys were denied that supreme delight and joy which accompanies stealing watermelons. One man did succeed in bringing a big striped watermelon all the way from Roseburg to Gold Beach in perfect condition. He was a squaw man. His woman was big and black and fat. He made her carry the melon in her lap the entire distance. Passing through villages, she put it under her apron.

Near the ocean melons will not mature, while up the river, the bear, deer, wild hogs, coons, and gophers all joined in raiding gardens, especially melon patches. Now Hathaway Jones craved watermelon more than anything else. He planted them year after year, always hoping he would discover some means for their protection. Ordinary fences were useless. There was a grove of young fir near the place. The trees grew thickly, were quite slim, and seventy feet tall. Hathaway cut these and built a fence of them, standing them on end, close together and pig-tight. In that fence were placed two thousand trees, and when it was finished, no deer could jump over it; but one night after the melon vines were just beginning to bloom, a bear pulled down a panel and the deer and wild hogs followed him into the patch.

One year Hathaway decided to sleep out in the middle of his melon patch. The experiment was a failure because he slept so soundly a herd of hogs rooted all around him and a gopher cut the roots of a vine which was growing within a foot of his head. He set a spring gun at the gap in the fence and shot his father's best mule. An Indian told him to dig a pitfall in the gap. This he did, covering it skillfully with sticks and leaves, after digging it ten feet deep. The very first night he heard something out by the trap, pulled on his boots, ran out to see what he had caught and fell into the pit with a big skunk.

Ten seasons he fertilized his ground, worked it well, planted his watermelon seed and waged losing battles with varmints. Then, just as he was commencing to feel a slight twinge of discouragement, a fisherman at Gold Beach gave him two hundred fathoms of gill net which was no longer strong enough to hold salmon, with the assurance that it would, if stretched around his melon patch, turn away all varmints.

Early the following spring Hathaway hauled all the mule fertilizer from the barn and scattered it upon his melon ground where he later plowed it under. He had repeated that job every spring until his father suggested he might be getting ready to sprout mules. Next the fish net was stretched around the field, tied to poles along the top, and pegged down at the bottom. He then made the hills and planted his watermelon seed.

Hathaway had never during the years before succeeded in getting his melon vines beyond the blooming stage on account of the pests which had always destroyed them. The sun warmed the earth and soon his plants were up and growing. His hopes and expectations grew also.

The wild creatures kept clear away from the net fence; even the gophers were afraid to dig under it, and the vines grew and grew. But when small melons formed, the vines dragged them along until they wore away. So Hathaway made a great number of sleds and put one under each small melon. That, however, did not help, as the vines just pulled the melons off the sleds. He then tied the sleds to the vines, and that worked until the melons grew heavy, then the vines would pull apart and go right on without the sleds or melons.

Hathaway sat up all night thinking and drinking moonshine, and toward morning figured out a system which could not fail. He put wheels on the sleds. He soon had to grease all the axles as they squeaked so loudly. All day long he would stand by the fence and watch the melons move around and grow. Within a couple weeks there were so many big melons they piled upon each other into mounds seven feet high.

That fall when the melons ripened they averaged three hundred pounds each. They were sweet as sugar and had small black seeds. People from all up and down the Rogue came for watermelons. Hathaway harvested fifty tons of melons from one acre of land. During the season he kept open house for all comers. Evenings he would plug some melons and pour into each a gallon of moonshine and the following day his visitors would remark that the melons were delicious and very invigorating.

The Watermelon Money

The fall Hathaway Jones raised his record crop of watermelons he stayed home and ate melon all day long and sometimes far into the night. Visitors were welcome to eat all they could, free. They only paid for what they carried away. Two watermelons made a good pack for a horse, one on each side. Hathaway charged two bits apiece for the ones he sold, but most of the purchasers merely promised to pay, knowing he would forget all about it.

By the middle of October a substantial portion of the second crop had been picked and eaten, and then there came a heavy frost which spoiled the few remaining melons. Harvest being over, Hathaway pocketed the proceeds of his cash sales and journeyed to Gold Beach in quest of bright lights and convivial company. He found the company, also the big kerosene oil lamp which hung in the saloon. It was not a very bright light but it served its purpose well enough.

Hathaway was used to good moonshine corn liquor, so the stuff they served him over the bar in that saloon soon had him bewildered and he lost all his money in a poker game. The next morning he awakened with the sun shining in his face. He was down on the beach between two sand dunes.

He started for the saloon to get a "hair of the dog that bit him," but upon searching himself discovered he had no money. However, he continued to the barroom in the hope someone would "set 'em up." He was too green to ask the bartender for a bracer, but just hung around. It was not long before two "outsiders" came in, stood up to the bar and had drinks of whiskey. Paying no attention to Hathaway, they were getting ready for another drink when he edged up to the bar and began telling the bartender about a big bull elk he shot the day before.

He grew quite excited while telling how the old elk seemed to know what he was trying to do. Every time he was just ready to pull the trigger the elk would dodge. Hathaway waved his arms and talked fast until, out of the corner of his eye, he saw the strangers were interested. He then told how he finally drew a bead, pulled the trigger, and hit the old bull elk square between the "yours."

[79]

One of the strangers asked: "What's yours?"

"Whiskey," said Hathaway, reaching for the bottle and pouring himself a big drink, "same as yours."

The Raccoon Tree

Version I

One time Hathaway was out hunting coons. He found a hollow tree that appeared to be a favorite hideout for them. He ran the coons into this hollow log, a tall, broken-off tree, and every time he ran a coon in at the bottom it pushed another out the top.

Version II

There was a period of time between the World War and the depression during which coonskins were at a premium. Hearing about the high prices, Hathaway Jones decided he would make some money. Coon sign was everywhere, and he owned two dogs that would run anything from a chipmunk to a cougar. They were so smart they understood everything he said, and it only required a few minutes to make them understand he wanted to run coons. The dogs seemed to think it would be fun chasing coons, because just as soon as they grasped what was wanted, they laughed and frolicked around in a manner peculiar to dogs when they are pleased over something.

They soon jumped a couple of coons, taking after them with a great hullabaloo of barking and other sounds characteristic of hound dogs. Every few minutes they would start more coons which would join with the others until it grew into a regular coon exodus. All the coons ran in the same direction, and before long there were so many they were like a herd of sheep, only very much faster. Away they ran with Hathaway and the dogs right behind. He, being a good runner, experienced no difficulty in keeping pace with the hounds. The coons ran much faster than could be expected of such fat, chunky creatures.

The chase continued for five miles, and some of the old extra fat coons began tiring and lagging behind. They would have liked to climb a tree, but there was no time. It looked bad for those old ones because the dogs were catching up, and, while coons can fight like demons, they cannot make a very good showing when exhausted from too much running. They were saved, however, from dog fighting by a big old red cedar snag which stood near the river in the middle of a small clear space.

The snag was fifteen feet in diameter at the ground and was eighty feet tall, and hollow. There was a small opening at the bottom, and, of course, the top where the tree had broken off was open. Coming into sight of the snag, Hathaway stopped and almost held his breath in amazement at what he saw. All the coons were running into the bottom of the snag. In their haste they crowded like people when they are panicky, or when they all want the same thing, and just as the old liver-colored lead hound was reaching out to snap him in his rear, the last coon darted into the snag. The dog tried to get in too, but the entrance hole was so small he could not squeeze through.

Now Hathaway knew he had a great many coons in the snag, but how to get their skins was a problem. It would take too long to chop down the snag, not to mention the hard work involved in that operation. Furthermore, when the snag fell, the coons might all run out and escape, unless the fall should smash the snag, but in that event the fur would probably be damaged. He thought of building a fire in the bottom of the snag and smoking them out, but a fire might burn up through the snag like a chimney and singe all the fur. Building fires in old snags was one of Hathaway's main sources of amusement, and he knew how fire is apt to roar up through them.

He considered chopping the entrance hole larger and climbing up into the snag, but he would need a ladder for that, the hollow part being quite large. Even if he succeeded in climbing up inside the snag the coons could escape him, as climbing would require both hands, leaving him nothing with which to catch them. It looked rather dark for Hathaway, but bright for the coons, when suddenly three big coons came running out of the woods with the hound dogs right behind them. They streaked for the snag and into the hole, but when they did so, a coon was pushed out from the top and was stunned by its fall to the ground. Hathaway finished it by hitting it on the head with a manzanita club, then sat down upon an old log and concentrated.

After a few minutes had passed, here came the dogs with three more coons, and, when they crowded into the bottom

of the snag, three other coons fell out of the top. Dispatching those three, he carried them to his log seat and there it dawned upon him that the snag was full of coons. So full that for every one that crowded into the bottom, one was pushed out of the top.

Day after day, and night after night, the hounds chased in coons, while Hathaway knocked on the heads and skinned the overflow. When the dogs grew hungry he fed them coon meat; and when he grew hungry he broiled coon backstrap on the end of a stick. While the dogs were hunting coons, Hathaway slept, and while Hathaway skinned coons, the dogs slept.

At last the dogs could find no more coons to round up, so they came and sat down with Hathaway, telling him by their expressions and actions they were all through. They had done well. The pile of skins had grown quite large, but the snag was full of coons and it seemed a shame not to get their skins.

So Hathaway told the dogs to go drive in a big mean skunk. But they hesitated, because there is nothing in the world a hound dog dislikes more than a skunk, except a porcupine, and it was only after he explained his reasons for wanting a skunk that they agreed and trotted away into the woods.

They were hardly any time at all finding a big skunk they could drive. Evidently the varmint knew about the old snag because he made for it as hard as he could run, which was not very fast. However, the hounds pretended that they could not catch him, keeping just a few feet behind baying and yelping at a great rate.

Gaining the hole in the bottom of the snag, the skunk decided to stop running and resort to chemical warfare. He released a blast of liquid gas hoping to catch the dogs on their noses, but the draft drew all the smell up through the hollow snag.

It was too much for the coons. They fairly streamed out of the top and rained down upon Hathaway and the dogs. Working furiously, they succeeded in killing them all, leaving the skunk in full possession of the snag; the dogs went to sleep, while Hathaway skinned and skinned, until, finishing with the last coon, he counted up and discovered that he had 7,581 prime skins.

The Slow Bullet

Version I

Smokeless powder had been introduced and Hathaway bought a box of cartridges loaded with it. Having been told the new powder was a great deal more powerful than black powder and much faster, he started out into the mountains determined to kill an old buck he had been trying to bag for years.

Most any morning the wise old deer could be seen browsing around a small bench far up on a mountainside. There was no way to get closer than one half mile without being seen by the buck, and with the first sight of Hathaway it would just vanish. He tried elevating his sights but could not even scare the buck unless he showed himself.

On this morning he gained the point of nearest approach without being seen, and, taking a rest on a boulder, aimed carefully and fired. He then discovered, greatly to his disgust, that he had forgotten to throw out the old black powder shells and reload with the ones containing smokeless powder. But when the smoke cleared away the old buck was still going about eating his breakfast indifferent to the shot.

Hathaway substituted the new for the old shells, once again took careful aim and fired, and the deer dropped dead in his tracks. He hurried up the mountain to inspect and dress his kill, feeling very much elated over having at last fooled the wise old buck. Arriving at the place, he drew his knife and bent over to bleed the deer when something stung him awfully hard in the seat of his pants. He thought a bald-headed hornet had hit him so he slapped that part of himself briskly, hoping to kill the insect, but what his hand found was the bullet from the black powder shell he had first fired. It had just reached the place.

Version II

One morning Hathaway stepped to his back door to throw out the dishwater when, glancing up the mountain across the canyon, he saw a big buck standing upon a high point of rocks. It was about two miles away, but he could see it clearly, could even count all five points on each of its horns. The air was very clear that morning.

Needing meat, he fetched out Old Betsy, took a rest across the back fence, and fired a shot at the buck. But after the smoke blew away he saw the buck still standing there as unconcerned as though nothing had happened. Then, seeking to reload for another shot, he discovered he was out of shells.

He stood there looking at the buck for quite a while, wondering what to do, when there flashed into his mind the fact that he had a small pistol which would shoot. Taking the pistol, he sneaked through the brush and up the mountain until he gained a position which was not more than twenty feet from the buck. Aiming the pistol with great care, he was just pressing the trigger when "thud," the bullet from Old Betsy hit the deer and killed it dead.

The Remarkable Bullet

Version I

Hathaway was able to fire a slow bullet. One time he shot a deer that was running away from him. The deer kept dodging and dashing as it ran a circuitous route through the woods. When the animal finally fell, Hathaway found sixteen bullet holes in him—all from the same bullet that the deer kept running into!

Version II

Another of the group asked Hathaway about a deer that had been shot seven times. "Were you mad at that there forked horn, harelip, 'er was you feelin' you had too many cartridges?"

"Only shot 'em one time," snarled Hathaway. "Jumped 'im up in the open timber 'tother side of Skunk Cabbage Flat, and he lit out dodgin' trees like a bat out-a hell. Jest as he dodged a great big fir tree I shot 'im right through the heart, but he run quite a ways 'fore he drapped. Well sir, he run so fast, dodging trees this away and that away, my bullet jest went in and out in and out a-makin' all them holes."

Version III

One time Hathaway Jones was hunting away out back of Silver Peak. Along about nine o'clock in the morning he jumped a big buck that ran a quarter of a mile through brush which was so thick and high it could not be seen. Beyond the brush, however, there was a small open space twenty feet across through which the buck would have to pass, so Hathaway prepared to kill it right there.

Coming to the open space, the old buck rose into the air fifteen feet, intending to clear it with one bound, but while he was in the air, Hathaway shot him nine times, killing him dead. Asked how he accounted for all those bullet holes when he had shot only nine times, he said the first shot hit the deer in the head and started it spinning so fast the rest of the bullets "went in and out, in and out, in and out."

Old Betsy's Remarkable Shot

Hathaway Jones owned an old buffalo gun in which he used black powder cartridges. It was a very good gun. The bullets fired from it traveled slowly but arrived at their destination with terrific force. It was this gun he used the time he killed the honker goose which was so high it took all afternoon to fall.

He was eating his noonday meal when he heard, just faintly, some geese. Stepping to the door, he looked into the blue sky, but could not see the geese; so he pointed Old Betsy up toward the locality where he thought the geese should be, then pulled the trigger.

The sun was setting that evening, and he had forgotten all about shooting up into the sky, when suddenly there was a sort of rushing noise, and a big, fat honker goose crashed through the cabin roof. The bullet from Old Betsy had cut its head off slick as a whistle.

Hathaway's Poor Marksmanship

Version I

"There's a little drainage ditch runs through a field I was passing yesterday where a bunch of geese had lit. I didn't have

[89]

my shotgun with me, so I grabbed up my rifle and sneaked over where I could look right along the canal. Them geese all had their heads down, drinking. So I whistled and, sure enough, all the heads come up together. I thought I could get them right through the necks. Only just then I happened to hiccup, and all I got was a basketful of bills."

Version II

Hathaway was quite a marksman, but one time he got off a bad shot. He was out in a meadow with his 30-30 rifle. A flock of geese passed over, circled, then settled down in a ditch in that meadow. Hathaway saw them lining up in the water and aimed his rifle to shoot a number of them. Just as he fired he "pulled off just a bit." All he got for his efforts was a "basketful of bills."

The Hunting Hound

Hathaway was sitting on his porch at Illahe. His old hunting hound, the best dog that ever lived, was there with him. Hathaway proclaimed that his dog could follow tracks which were even days old. Once the hound was tracking a bear; he followed him for miles through the hills and had nearly caught his prey when he came to a plowed field at the Lucas place at Agness. The dog was unable to follow the tracks across the field, but the next year, when the field was again plowed, the dog got back on the scent and found the bear.

Towser and Nellie

A wealthy dog fancier and a big game hunter from Virginia engaged Hathaway Jones to guide him on a hunt through the Rogue mountains, he having heard there were grizzly bears with white faces roaming the wild, unfrequented crags and dark canyons of Curry County. Hathaway encouraged him in his belief by telling of several encounters which he had experienced with "bald-faced grizzlies," one of which he had shot until his ammunition was exhausted, and then ran for his life. At the time he was carrying his 38-55, and the bullets just bounced off the tough hide of the grizzly; but if he had been carrying "Old Betsy," his 45-70, he might have stopped him. He estimated that particular grizzly would weigh 1,500 pounds, possibly a ton.

The man from Virginia told Hathaway all about the elephants, rhinoceros, crocodiles, lions, and other things he had killed during his wanderings all over the face of the earth, and how the pack of ten Airedales he had brought along for the white-faced grizzlies had actually killed several lions. He was not worried about his Airedales being able to take care of any bear that lived, and he knew his elephant gun would drop a grizzly in his tracks.

Hathaway explained that it would take at least three days for them to come to grizzly country, but that on the way the Airedales would probably have a chance to practice on a few common black ones, some of which were fairly good fighters. The sport agreed that it might be fun for the Airedales to tear a few small bears to pieces, a suggestion which Hathaway passed with the remark, "they are your dogs."

Leaving Battle Bar early in the morning, they hunted in the general direction of the Illinois River. Soon they saw an old she-bear eating acorns under a large white oak tree, and she saw them too. Away she went, lumbering down the mountain with her front feet trying without success to keep ahead of her hind feet. She crashed through brush, rolled over and over, tumbled over a cliff striking the ground thirty feet below with a thud. The fall, however, did not bother her; she just bounced up and ran away.

Several minutes were lost in finding a place where they could descend the cliff, but eventually the dogs were in full cry again. In the meantime the old bear had recovered from her panic and decided upon what she should do. She led her pursuers through tangled brush and white thorn, around dangerous bluffs, and up steep mountains, gradually drawing the Airedales away from the men. Then, deciding the time was right, she turned at bay in an alcove formed by some large boulders. Sitting in that place she was protected from the dogs on all sides except in front.

There are no braver dogs than Airedales. When they sighted their quarry, they rushed in to fight, for that is the way with Airedales and that was just what the old bear wanted. By the time the men arrived upon the scene the fight was all over. All of the Airedales had been slapped or hugged to death, and the bear was disappearing over a nearby ridge.

The owner of the Airedales was surprised, bewildered,

very sad, but also full of wrath. Hathaway explained what had happened—how the dogs, because of their bravery, had been victimized by the wiles of the old bear, and offered to return home, fetch his two hound dogs, Towser and Nellie, run it down, and kill it.

Leaving the man from Virginia sitting among his dead pets, crying like a child, Hathaway returned to his cabin for Towser and Nellie, and soon had them on the track of the bear. She once again came to bay in a place of rocky protection, but she could not slap nor hug those dogs. They just held her there until the men came and shot her. So impressed was the big game hunter he offered Hathaway $1,000 for his dogs. That is a lot of money for a mountain man, so after warning the purchaser to beware, because both dogs were dangerous, he made the deal.

Towser was all tan with yellow eyes, while Nellie was all jet black with green eyes. Hathaway sat down, took one of them under each arm and explained that they were to go with the other man, and that he would be good to them. They understood him too, but they growled their dislike of the idea. They refused to even notice the other man except to growl at him and show their teeth.

The next morning they put muzzles on both dogs, fastened them together with a short chain to their collars, tied a length of rope to the chain, and the man from Virginia led them away. They followed along with heads and tails drooping, and howling dismally.

Three weeks later Hathaway received a letter from Virginia. Towser and Nellie had escaped, and they were unable to find them. Their new owner had experienced a hectic trip home. Several people, including himself, had been bitten, and the hounds had howled and screamed with a weirdness that gave people the creeps. At last he turned them over to the keeper of his kennels, and Nellie promptly bit the man through the calf of his leg. They turned the hounds loose in a corral which was enclosed with an eight-foot fence, and closed the gate. It took Towser and Nellie a few minutes to discover they were free from chains and ropes, then over the fence they leaped as easily as though it had been no more than a foot high.

One dark night just two years later Hathaway was sitting alone in his cabin, thinking of Towser and Nellie, and wishing he had not sold them. He missed them every day, and could not endure having any other dogs around. It was the second anniversary of their parting, and he was quite blue. Suddenly there came riding down the night air the long-drawn-out hunting call of Towser, and while the echoes were still answering, he heard the wild screaming of Nellie. Soon there was a chorus that sounded like a great pack in full cry.

Hathaway stood in his door listening, and wondering what hounds there could be that sounded just like Towser and Nellie. They rapidly drew nearer, then out of the darkness old Towser came with a bound. Nellie was right behind him, and back of her came six more big black-and-tan hounds.

They all crowded into the cabin where the two old dogs all but smothered Hathaway with affection, while the other six stood at attention. He fed them all, then examined the young dogs. There were three males, and they each had a yellow right eye and a green left eye, while the three females each had a green right eye and a yellow left eye. The old dogs had taken two years on their journey back to the Rogue, and had raised a family en route. This was the pack of hounds that made Hathaway Jones the most famous hunting guide on the Rogue.

The Flying Bear

One year the huckleberry crop on the Rogue was so heavy the bushes drooped with the weight of their luscious fruit. In the woods the blue kind were almost as large as small cherries. So one morning Hathaway Jones decided he would gather a few and make a pie or two. He wandered up the mountainside back of his cabin, picking a few here, a few there, caring not at all how long it would take to fill his pail.

Now it happened that upon that very same morning a bear chose the same district in which to fill his stomach with those blue huckleberries. They met on opposite sides of a bush, each in his own way, showing surprise. Hathaway was totally unarmed, so he spoke to the bear, tipped his hat to him, and tried all the other things he could remember that are supposed to cause wild animals to go away and leave folk alone. The bear, however, did not seem to take to the idea. Instead of walking away with his stumpy tail between his legs, he gave a fierce growl and charged.

Hathaway ran. He knew the bear could catch him if he ran either up or down hill, so he ran around the mountain on the level. Running that way gravitation and the bear's weight would cause it to lose elevation and run below its quarry. The

bear, however, following a game trail, kept up a pace which made Hathaway extend himself. Everything, however, would have ended all right had not he come to a precipice and that stopped his going.

The bear by now was right behind him, so he climbed a tall, slim fir tree. The bear climbed the tree too. Up they went. They got so high the tree began to bend. Soon, with Hathaway right in the tiptop, the tree bent so far he jumped out. Relieved of his weight, the tree snapped back, throwing the bear far out into the air and across the canyon which at that point is a mile wide. Here he landed in another tall, slim fir tree.

The tree swayed back from the weight of the sudden force, then whipped forward and threw the bear across the canyon back into the first tree. Then away he went, and then again, all greatly to the amusement of Hathaway who sat down and watched him on his flying trips, as in the air the bear stretched out his neck and spread his legs like a flying squirrel.

Finally tiring of watching the bear in his air "tyration," Hathaway fetched an ax from his cabin and, while the critter was flying, chopped down the young fir tree that fell when the bear was about halfway back on the return trip. Seeing the tree gone, it changed its course and landed in a larger tree, off to one side.

The larger tree was much stronger than the tree Hathaway had cut down. It threw the bear clear over the top of the small tree he had been using on the other side into a still larger and stronger tree. That tree threw the bear back away over the top of the big tree on Hathaway's side into a still larger and stronger tree. And so it went, back and forth. Each trip the bear chose a taller and stronger tree, until passing through the air, he looked no bigger than a bobtailed mouse. Then, finally, an extra big tree on Hathaway's side threw the bear clear over the top of the mountain. The mountain was 4,000 feet high.

A stranger, standing around the Post Office at Agness and hearing Hathaway tell this experience, practically told him he was a liar, whereat Hathaway, curling up one side of his harelip, looked the stranger over and then with patience and condescension answered: "Wouldn't expect a tenderfoot to believe me, but I can take you to the young fir tree I chopped down. What better proof would a man with any sense want?"

Hathaway Out-Climbs The Bear

Riding along through a sleepy fall day, with his string of pack mules following around the winding trail like a long snake, Hathaway Jones passed Bear Camp at two o'clock in the afternoon. He was ahead of his schedule by nearly a minute. Here and there were his marks on the trees that showed the hour and minute he should be passing, if on time. Faring along wrapt in indifference born of native irresponsibility, he was suddenly jerked to attention by the sight of a bear coming down the trail from the opposite direction.

Pulling his rifle out of the boot, where he always carried it with him on his packing trips, Hathaway jumped off his horse and shot the bear with his 38-55, then, leaning his 45-70 against a boulder, he prepared to dress the animal.

At that moment another bear, as big as the first one and that was the biggest bear he had ever seen, came crashing through the brush. Then Hathaway noticed that his horse with his rifle in the boot had stampeded and was now half a mile away.

Two tall red cedars nearby grew quite close together. A hundred feet up a small limb from one reached across to the other. Hathaway climbed one of the trees, the bear following him. Hathaway crawled across the small limb into the other tree. The bear, testing the limb, decided it would not hold him, so he slid down and climbed the other tree, whereupon Hathaway crawled back to the first tree from where he jeered at the bear, shaking his fist and making faces but, once again, the bear slid down and climbed the first tree.

The bear continued climbing up and sliding down for two days and nights until his claws were worn to the quick, but always Hathaway escaped by way of the small limb; then the bear lost interest and started hobbling away on his sore feet. Hathaway watched the bear, and just as soon as its back was turned, climbed down, snatched up Old Betsy and shot him.

The Bear Hunt

Old Baldy Criteser and Hathaway Jones were hunting partners for many years, and it was quite a treat to hear them talk and argue about their experiences, especially when moonshine was plentiful. Baldy never tired of telling about the bear that chased Hathaway out onto a limb.

Hathaway had shot and wounded the bear and it charged him while he was trying to remove a shell which had jammed. The shell stuck, so Hathaway dropped his rifle and climbed a tall tree which grew on the edge of a 500-foot cliff, while the bear climbed right after him. Up a hundred feet there was a long space where there were no limbs, and Hathaway could climb no farther, but there was a long limb extending out over the cliff, and he crawled out upon it.

The bear climbed out on the limb too, while Hathaway begged him to go back. Baldy sat on the ground enjoying the show with never a thought of shooting the bear. Hathaway tried persuasion, then cussing, then threats, until he had crawled to the very tip of the limb from which there was a drop of 600 feet. The limb was bending dangerously but the bear kept coming. Finally Hathaway in desperation screamed: "Go back, you damn fool! This limb will break and we will both get killed!"

The Bear and the Honey Tree

Hathaway found that a bear had been raiding his honey tree. To remedy this loss of his honey, Jones hung a large boulder on a rope so that it closed the entrance to the bee tree. The old bear showed up to get his fill of honey and found the boulder across the entrance. He shoved the rock aside and reached in. The rock swept back and hit him. In anger the bear thrust the rock aside and reached in for more honey. Each time the rock hit him he got madder and each time he got angrier. Finally he shoved it away with so strong a push that the boulder swept around the tree and hit him in the head. Hathaway then walked up and hauled away the bear that had killed itself.

The Bear and the Bees

Hathaway Jones liked honey so well he spent a great deal of time hunting bee trees. But it was real work following bees over the mountains to their trees, and then the job of cutting down the trees was not to his taste, especially the large ones, some of which were four or five feet through. Having their trees cut down seemed to aggravate the bees too, and they would sting him until he fairly danced a jig between strokes of his ax.

Running out of honey, he would pit his memory of bee stings against his craving for sweets, and before long he would find himself chopping down a tree with the bees crawling up his pants legs and down his neck, all seemingly anxious to get rid of their stingers.

One time an old prospector stopped overnight with Hathaway who was all covered with swollen places from bee stings, and he told him how to catch bees and also how to make beehives. So the following spring Hathaway caught several swarms and hived them. Wherever he went he carried an old kerosene oilcan upon which he would beat furiously whenever he heard a swarm of bees traveling. The din would cause the bees to collect upon a limb where he could capture them and put them in a hive.

Eventually Hathaway had a dozen hives of bees of which he was very proud. The hives were made of sugar pine boards which he had first split out, then planed to an even thickness, an undertaking which entailed patience and some skill. The bees settled down in their nice homes and went right to work. Among the many other flowers there was an abundance of grizzly bear brush, azalea, wild lilac, and madrona, so the bees thrived and produced great quantities of fine white honey.

But one night during the second summer of his bee culture, and while he happened to be away from home, a big old bear smashed all the hives and ate all the honey together with most of the bees. Upon his return home Hathaway was sorely vexed. So possessed with the spirit of revenge did he become that he determined to kill that bear; besides he needed some fat for frying purposes.

Turning loose his hound dogs, he forthwith started the hunt. It was not much of a hunt at that because the old bear was so full of comb honey and bees he had only traveled a short distance before curling up by a log for a long sleep. Soon the dogs awakened him and bayed him against the base of a cliff where Hathaway shot him without the slightest compunction.

After telling the dead bear what he thought of him, Hathaway threw him across his shoulder and carried him home. And out of that old bear, besides all the meat, he recovered twenty-one gallons of lard and sixty-seven pounds of beeswax.

The Two Hungry Bears

Version I

One day Hathaway was out hunting and he killed a deer. Just as he was approaching the dead deer, he saw two bears rushing toward him, one from either side. He backed up to see what would happen. The bears began fighting for the meat. One took a swipe at the other; the other did the same. Their fighting continued until one jumped on top of the other; then the second bear did the same. They got to going so fast that they raised up off the ground. Finally the bears disappeared up into the sky. Hathaway said that it rained fur for three days.

Version II

Nope, [said Hathaway,] cougar and deer can move pretty spry when there's a need, but for real speed I'll lay my bets on bear, every time. I've seen a bear move so fast . . . well, I was back south of Collier's Bar just last March. The snow was goin' off pretty fast and the water was up. I aimed to get in a little ground sluicing on a right nice bar up that way. But I had to get camp meat, and was prowling along through a prairie when I ran onto the durndest sight. A cougar musta killed the night before, and the carcass of the towhead lay at the other end of the clearing. A big bear, gaunt and lean from his winter's hole-up, was makin' the best of the sitsashun, when another bear came out of the buck-brush and started in on the other end of the deer. Well, an argyment developed mighty quick; the first bear took a swipe at the second, and pretty soon they were really mixing it. One would get knocked sideways, and then he would dash in and jump on tother and tie into him, and then tother would jump onto the first, and then first onto tother . . . they got to moving so fast, one on top of tother, that they just natcherly went straight up and outa sight . . . all you could see afterwards was little bits of fur floating down with a splatter of blood, now and then. Never did know which one won.

The Trials of Hathaway

Version I

"My wife Florey said to me," Hathaway would begin, " 'you better go out and shoot us a deer. We haven't got a bit of meat in the cabin for breakfast.' " I hadn't gone but a little piece before I shot a five-hundred-pound bear. That bear was the fattest thing you ever saw. The grease run right out

the bullet hole and down the hill for fifty feet. Well, I threw him on my mule and started home. Part way along I come across a deer. So I shot him, too, threw him up on top the bear and packed on down to the river. And then that durned old mule balked. Seeing how I couldn't get him to cross, I threw the deer and the bear on my back and started swimming. Halfway over, I noticed I was swimming deeper than usual, and I looked around. You know, that darned mule was setting upon top the bear.

Version II

One day whilst I was riding up the trail on the Rogue, I spotted me a big bear acrost the river feeding on salmon. I shot the bear. I had me a pestle-tailed mule that was bigger and onerier than most. I tied my saddle horse to a tree, climbed onto the packsaddle and swam the mule tother side. I tied the bear on the mule's packsaddle and started back acrost the river, but that pesky mule balked at swimming. I couldn't budge him. I had to get that bear acrost the river. So I took it off the mule and started to swim with the bear on my back. About halfway over, I thought I was swimming pretty deep in the water. I looked up and saw that darned mule had climbed on top of the bear.

Independent Mules

Version I

Seems he had been working the string pretty hard for a week, and on Saturday night when he camped at Halfway Prairie, he made the mistake of telling the mules they was goin' to work the next day. "So, come daylight Sunday mornin' I couldn't hear the bell on ole Sue. It were a big loud bell what could be heered fer a mile 'er maybe two."

Hathaway searched for his mules without results until afternoon. Finally abandoning the search for a while he decided to go into the timber near the prairie to look for possible game to shoot. Suddenly he spotted one of his mules peeking out of the timber, looking around, rushing out to the prairie to grab a mouthful of grass and then rushing back again. He watched and saw other mules from the string repeat the process, but never "ole Sue." "So I snuck up where I could see what they wuz up to. There were ole Sue with her bell laying on a log so it couldn't make a noise, while the rest of the string of mules carried her grass to eat."

Version II

Toward evening Hathaway Jones arrived from Illahe with his mule pack train, and, after stabling and feeding the animals, proceeded to sample the "moon." Someone asked him what he considered were the smartest animals, and without a moment's hesitation he answered: "Mules are the smartest; jackasses are next; men are third."

Then, by way of illustration, he told them of an experience he had with his mules during the previous summer. He was packing heavy mining machinery from Agness to Mule Creek and his employer was in a hurry to get started mining, so Hathaway worked his mules on Sunday. They protested in every way a mule could protest. They balked, bucked off packs, laid down, and one of them kicked at Hathaway.

Now at one place along the trail there was a large prairie where the grass was good, so he usually camped there overnight on his way upriver. The mules liked that, and after eating their evening feed of grain, would wander around and have a good time.

They always stayed in a herd and were easy to find because one of them carried a bell which could be heard in the mountains for a mile or more. However, on Monday morning following his Sunday's work, he could not hear the bell. He looked all day but could not find a mule. Toward evening he examined the trail, but there were no tracks upon it, so he knew the mules were not far away.

Next morning while walking in the shade of the timber to avoid the heat, he noticed a mule walking slowly out of the brush. The mule looked all around, then rushed out where the grass was high, grabbed a mouthful of it and hurried back into the woods. After a few minutes another mule did the same thing. This action continued, so Hathaway made his way quietly through the timber until he reached a place from which he could see all of his mules. The bell mule was lying down in a way which prevented the bell from giving off any sound, and the other mules were carrying her grass to eat.

Hathaway's Old Mule

Charley Pettinger of Big Bend Ranch, Illahe, had the contract carrying the mail from Agness to all points east along the Rogue, and a great portion of the time he employed Hathaway Jones, he being quite skillful with packing and handling mules. The mail, including Parcel Post, and whatever freight there happened to be from time to time, was carried over a trail which, although it was called the river trail, nevertheless wound up and over every mountain its original surveyors could find. And, though they overlooked a few, they were small ones, mere hills.

Among the numerous mules which were used in the train were two very large and exceptionally tall greys which were such perfect mates it was hard to tell them apart. One was strictly a pack mule and could not be ridden; the other was strictly a riding mule and could not be packed. Hathaway talked to the mules just as he would to human beings, and the mules all understood and liked him because he was kind to them. They did not know what it was to be whipped, overpacked, or hurt while he was handling them. The big barn at the home ranch was headquarters.

[109]

One morning Hathaway cinched the packsaddles on the whole string, as he expected a heavy shipment of Parcel Post from the boat at Agness, but put his riding saddle on the wrong grey mule. Leading him out of the barn he swung into the saddle. Instantly the mule gave a big heave and Hathaway hit the ground hard, in a sitting position.

The fall jolted him badly, and caused him to lose his temper. Getting painfully to his feet, he stormed at the mule, "What's the matter with you, you old fool? Don't you know I have rheumatism?"

Hathaway's Worthless Mule

Hathaway came into Agness one day and overheard several of the men talking about the value of their mules. Finally they turned to Hathaway and asked him if his mule was a good one. Hathaway said, "No, it is not. In fact, the most he ever carried was a plow, a disk, and a harrow."

Hathaway's Remarkable Mule

[Talking to a dude in Gold Beach,] Hathaway said he walked very little, usually riding his little mule Sally whenever he went any place. She followed him around just like a dog, and she was quick as a cat.

He told the dude that he was, just the other day, riding Sally on the narrow trail around the cliff above the Devil's Stairway when they came face to face with a big hydrophobia cougar. The mad varmint was snapping its teeth together and snarling, while great gobs of froth flew out of its mouth. He was carrying his rifle across the saddle in front, but before he could even move, Sally turned a flip-flop and lit running the other way. She jumped so high the top of his hat just brushed the ground as she turned in the air, and there he was with his rifle still across the saddle, going the other way lickety-split.

The Red-Hot Mule

During the many winters Hathaway Jones worked at carrying mail over the Rogue River Trail and on to West Fork over Nine Mile Mountain, he was at times confronted with what, to a less ingenious man, would have been insurmountable obstacles caused by the convulsions of nature. Some winters it would rain ceaselessly for months, not just ordinary rain, but torrential downpours. The trail would be covered for miles with landslides, and even where it was clear, the pack mules would sink almost to their bellies into the mud and slush. These were the winters Hathaway called mild.

Other winters it would be cold, and instead of rain there would be snow. Great flakes, large as a man's hand, or blizzards, when the wind would scream and whistle and almost freeze him, swept the region. During the windstorms great snowdrifts would form, but Hathaway took it all in the day's work, sure of his ability to get through.

One cold day following a blizzard he came to a drift which was so big and high the mules could not, experienced drift climbers though they were, negotiate. There was no way around the drift, and he observed from a tree which he climbed, that it was fully half a mile across. Between drifts the trail and large spaces on either side had been blown clear of snow, and in one of these spaces there stood a large sugar pine tree.

Hathaway knew what to do. Stripping the saddle off his fast riding mule, he led her over to the pine tree and started her running round and round it. He kept talking to her and she kept increasing her speed faster and faster, round and round, until she was just a blur; then she became red-hot. Whereupon he drove her through the drift where she melted a passage-way for the pack train which followed.

The Hot Weather

Version I

Jones said he could tell about hot weather! A mouse came out from under his porch one day. It was so hot that the mouse could just barely move; it backed up under the porch again. Then it made a second try to get out into the yard—it could move only so slowly. Finally the mouse just stopped. The weather was so hot that the mouse fried to death and vanished right there.

Version II

One day Hathaway came into Agness from a trip down from Paradise Bar. He told everyone that although it was hot at Agness it was even more so up at Paradise. When asked how he knew so, he told of watching a lizard in the shade under a porch at a cabin at Paradise. The lizard wanted to reach a stump out in front of the cabin. Every once in a while it would edge out of the shade to run to the stump but the heat drove it back. Finally the lizard took off on the run to the stump but did not make it—he curled up and died, for it was too hot to make it that far.

Version III

One hot day during August, Hathaway Jones was sitting on the porch of the trail hotel at Big Bend Ranch near Illahe talking to Sadie Pettinger, the hostess, when she remarked that it was "awful hot."

"Oh yes," agreed Hathaway, "but this is cool compared to the heat at Paradise Bar." He said he was sitting in the shade in front of his cabin a few days back when he observed a lizard walking back and forth in the shade of the house. It was looking at something on a stump which stood out in the yard about thirty feet away. Finally the lizard made a run for it, but the heat was so great out in the sunshine it shriveled up, turned black, and burned to death.

The Year of the Big Freeze

The year of the big freeze, ice on the Rogue at Battle Bar was so thick cattle and horses crossed the river upon it. It turned cold so suddenly, some wild creatures were surprised. Scattered here and there were salmon lying on the ice which quickly froze under them when they jumped into the air for the purpose of discovering how they were progressing upon their journey to the creek of their nativity. A big blue heron pecked at a frog which was sitting upon a rock under the water, and before it could withdraw its bill the ice froze around it and held the bird fast. Hathaway Jones chopped the ice away from the heron's bill with an ax, and when it straightened up it still had the frog, which it swallowed.

Thin ice on standing water, which is common on frosty mornings, was all Hathaway had ever before seen. His grandfather, Ike, had told him of thick ice which forms on some eastern lakes and rivers; how the people skate, and drive wagon trains upon it. Testing the ice on the Rogue, he discovered it would support him, so he decided to take a walk.

He was having a grand time sliding around, and sometimes

sitting down abruptly, never dreaming the ice might not be thick enough all along the river to stand his weight. Suddenly he broke through into the swift, cold water which carried him under the ice.

Swimming downstream with all his might in the hopes of seeing a hole in the ice through which he could crawl out, he was very glad he had practiced holding his breath. It was cold under the ice, and his heavy clothing and shoes weighted him down to the bottom of the river. There he saw a big Chinook salmon and grabbed it by the tail, knowing it would, when scared, swim downstream.

The salmon darted away like an arrow from a long bow, towing Hathaway through the water so fast the friction warmed him. He enjoyed the speed and the warm glow which suffused him, but was at a loss to know how he would breathe after tiring of holding his breath.

Now Hathaway knew that salmon desiring to rid themselves of hooks or other undesirable obstacles usually leap high out of the water and shake their heads. He was thinking of that very thing when the fish whose tail he was holding saw a hole in the ice and leaped with all its strength. It was a big salmon, and a strong one. It leaped so high it landed upon the ice beyond the hole, dragging Hathaway out with it.

Whereupon he threw the salmon across his shoulders and carried it home for supper, helping himself along with a straight stick which he found by the trail. Arriving at the cabin, he leaned the stick against the wall back of the stove where the heat thawed it, and it turned out to be a snake.

The Great Snow

During the winter of the big snow, shortly after the war, Hathaway Jones discovered, greatly to his surprise and mental discomfort, that he was unpopular with the folk whose mail he delivered, along his route between West Fork and Illahe. They spoke of him in terms disparaging, both in respect to his personal character and his ability as a mail carrier. They "cussed" him, abused him, and scorned him, in his absence, but to his face, they were friendly and cordial.

Probably he would have gone along all through life cherishing warm friendship and neighborliness for these scattered mountain people, had it not been for the big snow. They seldom received mail. Here and there a letter, every two or three years, "Monkey Ward's" catalogue each March, and during election years, a few circulars from candidates for office, yet, on each mail day, at each place, the whole family would be waiting on the trail by the mailbox. Most families consisted of the elders and flocks of children and dogs, but at some cabins there would be just an old man living alone. They were always, on the surface, glad to see Hathaway, and that made his disillusionment very depressing.

Hathaway spent the night at West Fork, expecting to ride his mule to Illahe the next day, but during the night there was a great fall of snow which was dry and light as down. By morning it was more than three feet deep at West Fork and falling so fast he knew it would be very deep in the mountains.

No use trying to ride, but the catalogues had arrived a month earlier than usual and the folk would be glad to get them. They were heavy, but he made them into a pack and struck out on foot for Illahe thirty miles away.

The snow was so light and fluffy he walked right through it just as if it were not there. It became deeper and deeper as he gained elevation. Before long it was up to his waist, then to his armpits, then to his head, and when just his hat showed above the snow he thought it would look funny if some one should see a hat going along over the snow.

Before long it became so deep it was far over his head. He enjoyed walking along the trail out of the storm which was raging up above. The going was easy. There was practically no resistance to the snow. After a while he came to a small box, and overhead, up on top of the snow, he could hear the people talking.

They called him names for being late. In fact, they said awful things about him. The oldest girl was especially sarcastic and belittling in her remarks. She imitated his manner of speaking, just as though he could help being born with a harelip. He had been thinking she were pretty nice too. Shoving a catalogue into their mailbox, he dismissed them from his mind as a shiftless, ne'er-do-well outfit, feeling sure he would, at the next place, hear a good word about himself.

But at the next place he heard them stamping around to keep their feet warm, while saying worse things than the others. It would have been a pleasant trip walking along deep under the snow out of the storm where it was nice and cool, making good time, too, but during the entire trip he heard not one good word about himself.

Reaching the lower level of the Big Bend Ranch at Illahe, where the snow became less deep, he walked out and came right face to face with an old squaw who was gathering fir bark. Hathaway said she took one look, then dropped her squaw wood and went away from there. "Old fat squaw run faster'n a horse!" he exclaimed.

The Lost Bacon and the Deep Snow

The trail over which mail and freight is transported from the middle and lower Rogue is just about like all such trails throughout the mountainous districts of the Old West. As long as pack animals can manage to travel, nothing in the way of repairs is ever done. Even trees which are always falling across trails are never cut away if it is possible to go around them. During the winter season packers experience great difficulty with landslides and deep snow.

Following snowstorms in the mountains, at elevations of 300 feet or more, a crust freezes over the surface of the snow. In exposed places the trees which grow up through it are swayed by the wind, and the bark becomes scored by the icy edges. After the snow is melted away, its depth of the previous winter can be accurately measured. There are several places in Curry County where snow marks on the fir trees are quite distinct. Along the trail between Snow Camp and Game Lake the snow scores on the trees furnish mute evidence of snow which was thirty feet deep, while north of Agness the snow-fall is even greater.

One winter, several miles east of Mule Creek, Hathaway Jones was traveling along through a blinding snowstorm with a pack train of ten mules, all loaded with general merchandise. It had been snowing for days. The flakes were as big as a man's hand, and came so thick he was compelled to shovel it off the mules every few minutes to keep them from being buried alive. At one place the trail rounded a hogback where the mountainside was very steep. Only a hundred feet below, the Rogue, which was high at that time, was raring and raging through the canyon. Scattered here and there were pine trees, some of which were entirely buried beneath the snow, while the weighted-down tops of others could still be seen. The trail was somewhere away down under the snow, and Hathaway was forced to depend entirely upon the sagacity of the mules.

Suddenly one of the mules lost its footing and went falling and rolling down the mountainside until it eventually plunged into the turgid river and was swept away. The rope which formed the diamond hitch snapped when the mule first rolled over, the whole pack came apart, and the various articles it contained were scattered down the mountain. There being nothing Hathaway could do about it, he continued upon his way, but the owner of the goods made some remark about his ability as a packer, so he quit the job.

During the month of August four years later Hathaway just happened to be riding along that trail, and, coming to the place where the mule rolled into the river, he noticed a white object high up in a tall pine tree. He had all but forgotten the incident of the lost mule, and it did not occur to him, at the time, there could be anything in common between the white object and that unfortunate animal.

Being of an inquiring mind, Hathaway ground-reined his horse, and made his way down to the pine tree which he climbed. Fifty-one feet up in the tree, hanging on the snag of a broken limb, there was the side of bacon. His first impulse was to leave it alone, as he assumed it would have long since become spoiled, if not actually decayed. But he carried it down to the ground and removed the wrappings, and, as he said, "it was just as sweet and fresh as it was the day it left the store."

The Devil's Stairway

There is a place near the "Devil's Stairway" where the trail, for some distance, has been blasted through hard rock. The strata lies on edge and consists of a series of hard layers, two and one-half feet thick, between which there are layers of soft material one foot thick. Time and the elements have worn away the soft layers, leaving holes in the trail which are from eight to ten inches deep.

An Easterner was being packed in by Hathaway Jones for a big game hunt. Observing the holes in the trail, he asked Hathaway if he knew what had caused them. Without stopping to think he told the man that he had made them, and of course the Easterner wanted to know how they were made and for what purpose. But Hathaway, being unable to say, offhand, why he had made the holes, told the Easterner to remind him that evening in camp and he would tell him all about it.

During the rest of the afternoon Hathaway concentrated upon the subject. He was sorry, for a time, that he had claimed those holes in the trail. Realizing he should have thought up something about those holes long ago, he turned over in his mind several explanations, but none of them were satisfactory. And, right after camp was made and the evening meal was eaten, that Easterner expressed a desire to know about those trail holes.

So Hathaway, in his inimitable hare-lipped manner, and with a vocabulary which was startling, picturesque, and very effective, related to his "sport" how he made the holes in that hard rock.

Back on a ridge a few miles he shot a big fat buck. Only wishing one deer, he shouldered the buck and started for home. But another big buck stepped from behind a bush and, without stopping to think, he shot it. Well, he guessed he could make jerky out of the extra buck, so he pitched it on top of the other and once again headed for home.

All would have been fine and easy except there were big bucks all around. He forgot he had use for only one deer. Of course they would not waste; he could use them. But, even though there were big bucks standing around in herds, he stopped shooting as soon as he had seven big ones on his back.

Those seven bucks were the biggest and heaviest deer he

had ever carried. The weight on his back was a mere trifle, but it made walking hard. Coming to the hard rock trail he expected to get along faster, but the load he carried was so heavy he sunk in to his knees every step. "And there's the holes to prove it," asserted Hathaway.

The Broken Leg

The time Hathaway Jones broke his leg, the job of setting it fell to his father Sampson, aided by a younger brother. They were inexperienced in bonesetting because they always shot animals that had broken legs. They talked the matter over and agreed it might be best for all concerned if they shot Hathaway, but decided they would try patching him up.

Sampson, like most all mountain folk, had a "Doctor Book," probably a copy of the same one mentioned by Mark Twain because no one could read it without acquiring doleful forebodings concerning the state of his own health. But the book told all about bonesetting, and they tried to follow directions. The splints were easily made and bound into place after they had pulled the broken ends of the bones together. The "Doctor Book" said, however, that the leg should be put into a plaster cast, and they had no plaster.

Now folk who live several days' travel from the nearest doctor learn to solve many difficult problems. They had a sack of cement which they had packed in from Powers, intending to use it in curbing their spring. So, having no plaster, they mixed up a batch of cement out of which they contrived a very good cast for the broken leg.

A flea happened to be left under the cast, and even years afterward Hathaway would fly into a rage and pour out a stream of cuss words whenever any one mentioned that flea. When the time came for the removal of the cast from Hathaway's leg, Sampson used a single jack and a drill, while Hathaway watched for the flea. He saw it and made a grab, but the flea hopped onto a hound dog that was standing by and, mingling with the fleas that swarmed in the dog's hair, lost itself in the crowd.

Hathaway's Great Strength

Upon one of the rare visits to Gold Beach indulged in by Hathaway Jones he was accosted by a stranger, and a "dude" at that. He was pointed out to the city man who had been making inquiries respecting a Jones whose reputation had spread far and wide from the wilds of the lower Rogue, until whispers concerning him were beginning to be heard in the great cities throughout the land. Hathaway was young in years but old in the ways of the mountains. He was retiring and bashful in the presence of strangers, especially dudes whom he held in contempt. He did not respond in a cordial manner to the stranger's advances.

Ignoring the dude's proffered hand, Hathaway continued slowly toward the saloon, permitting the stranger to do all the talking. But when the man asked Hathaway if he could lead him to a place where they served good drinking liquor, the ice was broken, and over their drinks, which the stranger paid for, they soon became at ease with each other.

After the fifth or sixth drink the city man asked Hathaway where he was working, to which inquiry the latter answered that he never worked. "Why not?" pursued the stranger, with apologies for his temerity.

Hathaway merely answered: "Can't."

"Why not?" persevered the dude.

"'Tain't good for me," answered Hathaway.

"What does work do to you?" persisted the dude.

Whereupon Hathaway, helping himself to another drink for which the dude paid, stated that he was a mass of scars caused by his efforts to work; that he liked to work, and was very downhearted about his unfortunate condition. "Look at my gold mine," he declared in accents forlorn. "Boat load of gold a week if I could work, and here I am broke. Ranch work behind, wood to chop for winter, hogs to kill, dad old and weak, brothers all worthless, and all I can do is stand around like a wooden Indian."

"You look pretty strong and healthy," observed the stranger.

"Strong! Healthy! You bet I'm healthy and strong. I'm the strongest and healthiest man on the lower Rogue," exclaimed Hathaway.

"Then why can't you work?" queried the stranger.

So Hathaway explained that work was exercise, and that whenever he exercised his muscles developed so fast they split through the skin from one end to the other.

Gold in the Far Country

Version I

One day when he was a boy, Hathaway had been out mining. He found gold. It was so rich a strike that the gold was just hanging there in melted columns. Hathaway broke off a big section—so soft that it was like soap. He "took it to Pappy." His father asked him where he found it. Hathaway said that all that gold was "on the far side of Craggy Mountain." His Pappy's only reply was, "Well, son, that's too far from the railroad."

Version II

Sometime early in this century miners were developing claims at Mule Creek. These men often came to Agness talking about their mines. Hathaway said that he had found all these locations a long time before the newcomers had come into the country. Telling about it, he would say: "Well, it was like this. . . ." Hathaway had been out hunting with his father one time. While near Mule Creek he found gold so rich that he "could just bend it." Hathaway showed his discovery to his father and to his uncle too, but they dissuaded him from following up mining, for the gold, in their opinion, was "just too far from the railway."

Hathaway's Rich Lode

Version I

The reason for our prospecting about that location [Mule Creek] was that on one of his trips along the trail Matoon had picked up a piece of rock that we had assayed and got a test of $90 a ton in gold. We thought to find the ledge it came from, but never did. "So you didn't find your ledge," Hathaway remarked. "A year or so ago I was drilling some holes on the face of a ledge over on Cattle Creek, and I heard the bells on the 'animals' startin' out on the trail for home. I dropped everything and ran to head them off, and didn't get back to the ledge for a month or more. When I did come back the gold was just oozing out of the drill holes."

Version II

One evening when a group of old-timers was gathered together with a jug of moonshine and a stack of tin cups so all could help themselves, someone asked Hathaway about some holes he had drilled in a big ledge. Seems Hathaway had borrowed a single jack and drill, claiming he had discovered the biggest gold mine in the world.

"Din't I tell you 'boutin' them holes in that there ledge? I drilled 'em 'fore I brung back yer tools, but when I got home fer powder to blast 'em there weren't none. Paw done used it all up blastin' salmon down in the mouth of the crick. Sure raised hell with the salmon. Got 'nough to salt down a bar'l full. 'Twas a long time 'fore Paw got some powder brung up from Gold Beach.

Well, drilled them holes last May, an' went up to blast 'em out here about a week back, but when I come to 'em they weren't no room fer the powder. They was filled up with gold so the powder wouldn't go in. Gold were oozin' outen them holes and dreein' down the mountain plum t' the crick. Weren't nothin' I could do so I jest says to myself—to hell with 'em."

Version III

When Hathaway Jones was about twenty years of age he and another boy found a ledge of quartz which they decided was a good prospect. They borrowed a drill and a single jack, carried them to the ledge and drilled several holes the full length of the drill. They then tried to borrow some powder, but on account of their youth no one would trust them with explosives.

They were determined to blast the ledge, feeling sure they would uncover huge quantities of gold, so the following winter they trapped some mink, sold the skins and with the money thus obtained some sticks of dynamite, caps and fuse, and after the passage of nearly a year, started out to do their blasting.

But when they arrived at their ledge they discovered that gold was oozing out of the holes and running down over the rock like syrup. Discouraged because the holes they had drilled were all plugged up so they could not put in the dynamite, they abandoned the project, carried their dynamite to the top of the mountain, and set it off in one big blast just to hear the noise.

The Remarkable Watch

Version I

Legend has it that on one of his trips to Grants Pass, Hathaway purchased a new watch for himself. Since this was his first watch, he was very proud of it. On the return trip he sat down in the snow to eat, and hung the watch on a small fir tree so he could admire it while he ate. During the time he sat there his mind wandered to other things, and he walked off without his watch. Since he didn't miss it until much later, it wasn't possible for him to go back for it that trip.

The next summer he chanced to sit under a tall fir tree to rest. He heard a strange ticking sound, but couldn't find it by just looking around. Finally he determined it was coming from the tall fir under which he was sitting, so he proceeded to climb the tree to discover what manner of thing was making this queer ticking sound. What should he discover way up that tall tree but his long-lost watch still shining brightly and ticking like new!

Version II

One winter snow started early on the Rogue and came down so fast that Hathaway, hunting in the hills, couldn't walk out to his cabin and had to sit down and slide from the hilltop to the river bank. On the way down he lost his watch, which was a real pity as he had intended timing the slide. Next summer he was hunting in the hills again and sat down under a tree to rest. He became aware of a ticking sound near him which he finally located up the tree under which he was resting. He got up, climbed the tree, and there sure enough was his watch, still going. That was how he knew how deep the snow had been that winter. He climbed sixty feet up that tree.

Version III

And, of course, as was the occasion, and this has been pulled many times on many people, the pride the old-timers drew from having a good watch was unbounded. Hathaway Jones's father was no exception and when he died he left his watch to Hathaway Jones; it was one of his prized possessions. Unfortunately, one fall when Hathaway was hunting he lost this watch and much to his dismay could not find it. However, two years later while hunting in that same area,

Hathaway, well, let's let Hathaway tell it: "Here I was walking along the trail and I hear tick, tick, tick, tick, tick, and I looked around. You wouldn't believe this, but it was that watch still running away. Only lost two minutes in two years."

Version IV

While carrying the mail during one severe winter, Hathaway Jones stopped to rest upon the summit of Eight Mile Mountain, and while leaning against a tree, broke through the snow. When he attained the surface once more, after several hours of hard burrowing, it was growing late and he had many miles yet to travel before shelter could be found. Then reaching for his watch, he discovered it was lost. He might have frozen to death that night but for a bit of luck. An avalanche carried him six miles, clear to the bottom of the mountain, and almost home.

The following July he once again stopped to rest at the same place. He was sitting down eating his lunch under a tree when he became aware of a tick, tick, tick coming from somewhere overhead. So he climbed up the tree sixty feet and there found his watch ticking away, hanging on a limb. From that experience he knew the snow on Eight Mile Mountain had been sixty feet deep during the previous winter.

The Magnificent Fireplace

Version I

You'd ought to have some of the draft we had in the fire-place pa and me built in our cabin [said Hathaway]. We carried up a pile of big rocks and then mixed ashes and clay for mortar and put about a sack of salt in it. After we got the fireplace built we got a joint of big mine pipe for the chimney and I found a short piece of pipe that was littler at one end and put it on top like a nozzle. Pa says, "We'll let her dry out plenty 'fore we build any fire."

After we got the punchin' floor down, we started squarin' the walls with an adz. The floor was all piled full of chips, and pa says, "I'm goin' to scoop some of this stud into the fireplace and burn it so maybe we can find the floor."

The chips and shavings begun to burn right now, and she commenced to get hot. Perty soon she begins to suck and roar, and she started draggin' the chips off the floor and into the blaze. Pa and me run outside, and she sucked that cabin as clean as if we'd swept it.

Version II

Another thing that Hathaway Jones was proud of was his father, and he felt that his father was a real builder of fire-

places. Now in the old days, fireplaces were built with the one thing in mind, that was to draw good. Now a fireplace that 'drew good,' as they used the expression, meant that it did not smoke. The reason, of course, that it didn't smoke was that it drew in enough air from the surrounding room that the heat, usually, and the smoke all went up the fireplace chimney. One day—let us let Hathaway Jones tell it—his father had just completed a fireplace. Picture, if you will, an old ramshackle log cabin with a clapboard door, small porch outside to which was tied a hound dog, and you have the setting. Hathaway Jones tells it this way: "Pa, he built this fireplace and boy did that fireplace draw. You never seen a fireplace like that. He shut the door and built a fire in this fireplace and the first thing it did, it drew the door right off the hinges, sent it up the chimney. The old hound dog bitch was about to have puppies was tied to the post of the porch and then she came right behind that door; it pulled four pups right out of her and before we could put out the fire, we had two more! That's drawing."

Version III

The home in which Hathaway Jones was born, and in which he lived for several years after attaining voting age, had no open fireplace until he built one during the summer of his sixteenth year. While a small boy he frequently visited some of the few other homes within a radius of thirty miles; it was ten miles to the nearest neighbor, and in each of those houses he enjoyed sitting before an open fire. He had roasted apples on the hearths and eaten them half baked, had played in the fires with sticks, and fallen into one fireplace where he burned his hand. To him fireplaces were fascinating, comfortable, and very desirable.

Returning home from such visits to a house which was heated by a stove he would, for weeks, keep after his father to build a fireplace. But the old man always claimed he knew nothing about building with stone and mud; they could not obtain bricks, nor the material used in making mortar, nor would he build a chimney of mud and sticks for fear of fire hazard. He explained to the boy that even though all sorts of chunks, roots, and trash could be burned in a fireplace, the fact remained that in order to heat the house, a great deal more wood than the amount consumed by the stove would be needed.

Now Hathaway persisted, day after day, and year after year, until at the age of sixteen he gained permission to build a fireplace himself. His father insisted the boy could not build one that would draw, and that meant the house would be as full of smoke as an Indian dugout. The old man said that only experts could make fireplaces which would draw—men who had experience, so Hathaway set out to gain experience.

Out a short distance from the house there was an outcropping of sand rock which was in layers of different thicknesses. Hitching an old mule to a small sled, he went about hauling in rock. Having been told that four times more rock than the amount originally calculated was always required in rockwork, he hauled in six times more than he thought he could use, and, as it turned out, that was not one half enough.

Fortunately Hathaway was born with great talent respecting most everything. He planned his chimney and fireplace within his mind, and carried on the construction according to mental specifications. Several weeks of steady work, from dawn to dark, were consumed in building, and when the job was completed, it appeared to be well done. The boy had agreed to tear it down and repair the house unless it drew, and now it was ready for the test.

Gathering a handful of shavings from the floor where there were plenty, he placed them within the fireplace and started them burning with a match. The chimney began drawing with a roar. Soon the draft became so strong it sucked in all the chips and trash from the floor, sweeping it clean for the first time since the house was built thirty years before. Hathaway opened the back door to call his father in to see the fireplace draw, and the draft was so strong it commenced pulling sticks from the backyard, so he slammed the door shut.

The woodpile was out in the backyard, and, when he again opened the door, the draft began drawing in sticks of wood. His father, seeing that, came in and enjoyed the fire while talking things over. The upshot of it was that for years they hauled in and piled their firewood in the backyard, and whenever the fire needed replenishing they merely opened the back door and allowed the fireplace to draw in what wood was required.

Version IV

My old man and me, [said Hathaway,] we once built a cabin on Bald Ridge over on the Rogue. We used logs and poles handy about, and the old man took a lot of time hewing them to fit. When he finished, the front yard was all cluttered up with chips. I built the fireplace, but the old man wasn't happy with it. He said the chimney was too small and claimed it wouldn't draw. I claimed it would. When we finished the cabin, the old man built a fire to test the fireplace; but the darned old fool, he left the front door open. That fireplace cleared the whole front yard of chips.

The Rolling Stone

Version I

When he was building his house, he left a space right in the center of the stone fireplace for a rock of a certain shape and size which he fancied would look right. He couldn't find a rock to fit the place anywhere, and had just about given up, when one day out hunting he came on a big rock which seemed to him to have possibilities as to shape. He rolled the rock down the steep hillside, saw it roll up the opposite side, down again and back again—a pendulum swing. Satisfied, he went away down the Rogue, fished all summer, came back in the autumn and there was that rock still rolling. One quick look at it convinced him that it was now the right size. He hastily put a log under it, stopped its descent, took it home, and it was a perfect fit.

Version II

Hathaway found a big rock above him on the trail, a rock which he had seen many times. One day he feared that it would break loose and fall, so he took a big pry bar and hooked his mule to it and pulled. At last it came loose and came crashing down into the canyon and rolled to the top of the other side. He stood there and watched it roll back and forth from canyon wall to canyon wall. He at last decided that he had to go on and deliver his mail. When he returned he looked to see what had happened. Way down in the canyon he saw something moving. There was a small pebble rolling up the mountainside. That was all that was left of the boulder.

Version III

Seems Hathaway needed a round rock to complete the mantel on his famous fireplace, but search as he might he just couldn't find one the right size and shape. "Hunted till I was plum wore out, tryin' to find a round rock fer that there hole, so I decided to make me a round rock" [Hathaway said].

"I taken the crowbar and climbed up one side of Deep Canyon up yander, and right at the top I finds a big boulder what be a purty red."

"Took a lot'a prying to get'er started, but when she did, she went down the side 'a that there mountain, like hell beatin' tanbark. She took out up 'tother side, spinnin' and hummin' like a top. Soon as she gits as fer as she kin go over thar, back she comes, throwin' brush and trees 'round like feathers."

"Gettin' up to whar she started from, back she rolled. Well, sir, I jest set there an' watched 'er roll about a hundred trips, then seein' how she were doin' and thar she was, rollin' back and forth. You'd ort to'a seed her and heard 'er hum. She war wore round by that thar time. Every day I went an' looked 'til she wore down to jest the size fer the hole in that thar mantel, and she were round as a buck shot."

"Had me a leetle trouble ketchin' 'er, scopped 'er up in a sack, when she war passin'. Damned if'n she didn't keep right on spinnin' and hummin' all the way home, but soon's I got 'er in that hole, she kinder slowed down."

Version IV

"The deepest and steepest canyon in Curry County lies backcountry just south of the Craggies," announced Hathaway Jones, as he leaned forward to plant a sizzling brown jet in the heart of the campfire coals. "The walls on both sides run up well nigh three thousand feet on each side of the leetle creek which empties into Tincup creek a mile or so down-canyon."

He settled himself against the stump, and we knew we were in for another of "Hathaway's stories." "Ten-fifteen years ago, I was a-prospecting down that way, and happened to come along the ridge on the north of that particular canyon . . . it's a knife-edge ridge, and I was a-pickin' my way mighty slow, when I came on one of them big round boulders a-roostin' on the narrow ridge-top, like a fool hen on a log. It was balanced there so I could jiggle it with one hand, even tho' it was over eight feet high and musta weighed nigh on to ten ton. Yep . . . I did just what you'd a done . . . I put my back to it and heaved, and it teetered, and with another heave started to roll over, slow. It sure picked up speed, and before it'd gone a hundred yards, 'twas a-tearin' down the canyon-side bitin' out chunks of rock at each jump. By the time it

[139]

reached the bottom it was hittin' up such a pace it only made one splash in the creek and then bounded right up the other side of the canyon . . . almost to the top of the ridge . . . before it slowed down and started to roll back.

Them canyon walls were so steep and so smooth that that blamed boulder just kept a-rollin' back and forth, back and forth, not quite reachin' the top of the ridges on both sides. I watched it for nigh onto half an hour before I realized 'twas gettin' late and I'd better hit for camp." Hathaway took time out to replenish his quid, and after a moment in which we all thought, "Well, here it comes!" he remarked, with a twinkle in his eye, "Ye know, I was down to that same place last fall, just after the big fire, and durned if that boulder wasn't a-rollin' yet . . . only it had worn itself down so weren't no bigger'n your head."

Version V

Upon reaching the age of twenty-one, Hathaway Jones decided he should get married and raise a family. He was tired of washing his own clothes, raising a garden, and chopping wood; not to mention the plowing and other ranch work, including "slopping" the hogs. His father, Ike, told him that the first thing toward a felicitous matrimonial venture ought to be a house through the door of which he could carry his bride.

Selecting a place where the canyon widened a little, the young man set to work. It was a lovely spot by a fine spring where the sun shone even on the shortest of days of winter, when it shone at all. He cut and peeled enough logs, split out his shakes and went to work with a will.

It did not take very long to build the house, all but the chimney and fireplace upon which he worked for a long time. For the mantel he gathered different colored rocks from the river bars, and right in the middle he left a round hole for a centerpiece. He thought it would be a simple matter to find a pretty round rock which would fit the hole, as there were countless round rocks all along the river.

He searched the creek and river bars for several days, finding any number of round rocks, none of which would fit the hole, so he sat down under a tree and thought the matter over; and, while so doing, he conceived an idea out of which, after years of meditation, he worked out the demonstration of perpetual motion with which all are familiar. However, for the simple matter of providing a suitable rock for the hole in his mantel, he required only rudimentary knowledge respecting the great theory involved.

Climbing to the top of a high ridge, he selected a large boulder of red rock which was full of bright pyrites, and started it rolling down the mountain. Down it went, then up the other side, then back it came up to where it started, then down it rolled again, and so on.

Hathaway watched the rock roll until he was satisfied his idea was sound, then returned to his cabin and let it roll. Each morning he walked down the canyon and watched the rock go by on its regular trips. By the end of the second month the rock was perfectly round, and looked as though it might be getting down to about the right size, so after that he stopped, and measured it each morning, then turned it loose again. Finally, after about three months of rolling, the rock was worn down until it fitted the hole exactly.

The Seven-Foot Bread Loaf

Frequently due to reasoning which only Curry Countians could possibly understand, Hathaway walked to West Fork for supplies which he carried home on his back. Over the trail each year he packed many a load with his pack mules, but never once thought of using an empty animal to bring in provisions for the winter. Such was not the way it was done!

Many years ago, right in the dead of winter and with food getting low, Hathaway, disregarding six idle pack mules in his pasture, plus his riding mule, Sally, walked to West Fork. He made the trip over in one day, and started for home early the following morning. He carried, among other things, a 50-pound sack of flour. There was a promise of rain in the clouds, and before Hathaway could reach shelter, the rain started falling. There came a regular lower Rogue rain with drops so big and close they crowded each other into something resembling a waterfall.

Toward noon Hathaway gained the top of Nine Mile Mountain, and while he was warm due to walking up the mountain with a heavy pack on his back, he was wet as a "drowned rat." The rain had turned to snow, and Hathaway started looking for shelter. He finally found an overhanging cliff which frequently provided shelter for stormbound travelers who had no better sense than being there at all. Here he took off his pack, built a fire, then proceeded to dry his clothes while boiling coffee.

Standing close to the fire, he steamed, smoked, and smelled "like all git out." "You don't never ketch cold if'n yer dry yer clothes without taken 'em off," he always said.

The 50-pound sack of flour provided Hathaway with somewhat of a problem. It was soaking up water, and he just couldn't afford to lose it, so he decided the only solution was to bake it into bread right then and there.

He always carried with him an old-time gold pan which was almost as big as a common dishpan. He used it instead of his hat when watering his mule string from springs along the trail.

Mixing the flour into dough, he "set" it in the gold pan which he placed upon a bed of coals from the fire. Around the gold pan he raked up coals while the dough commenced to "raise."

As it raised, he raked up more coals. It raised and raised while Hathaway raked and raked, until when it was finally done to a lovely brown, he had a loaf of bread seven feet high.

Ticks in the Rogue Wilderness

Version I

One year on the lower Rogue there were so many ticks they became a deadly menace to the deer. There are no spotted ticks in this part of Oregon, but there are several kinds of ordinary ticks which usually are of no particular consequence. They seemed to concentrate upon some deer, while avoiding others, and they caused their victims to become thin and weak. Hunters could tell the ones which had ticks from the others as far as they could see them.

That year every one was covered with tick bites which, at certain stages, produce itching that just has to be scratched. One day Hathaway Jones picked up his rifle and started out to get a "piece of meat." He strolled along scratching himself here, and scratching himself there, occasionally picking off a tick, or scratching his back against a tree, until he arrived at a point which afforded a clear view of a low brush ridge where there were always deer.

And there, standing broadside to him, and within easy range, he saw a big buck which appeared to be in good order. He shot it, but it did not fall down. He shot it again, and again, but it just stood there, not even looking around. Walking toward it, he shot it every few steps, but the buck continued motionless.

Eventually he walked right up to the deer which he discovered was dead and dry. There remained just the skin stretched over the bones. The ticks had sucked out everything else, and it stood there with its mouth open so the wind kept it inflated and looking fat.

Version II

Hathaway said: "One day I come along here and there were seven deer in that little draw. One of them was black as coal. I had never seen a black deer, so I shot that one, and when I come up to him I see he was just a mass of fleas."

The Cow and the "Ole Wommin"

One individual, when asked about the tales of Hathaway, told his favorite (which has several versions). Seems Hathaway had a milk cow, and that milk cows were hard to come by in those days up the river. A friend had been trying to buy the cow from Hathaway, but had been unsuccessful. One day he decided to have another try, so he armed himself with a jug of moonshine and proceeded down the trail to Hathaway's cabin.

The pair drank moonshine and talked for hours, and Hathaway's "ole wommin" finally gave up and went to bed, leaving the two cronies to drink their "likker" and spin their yarns. When the moonshine was almost gone, Hathaway's friend told him he could imitate his odd way of talking and could convince the "ole wommin" that he was Hathaway.

Hathaway was just as sure that it couldn't be done, so he took his friend up on a bet—10 dollars against the milk cow. As soon as the bet was made, the friend went into the bedroom, took off his heavy boots, dropping them on the floor as was Hathaway's custom.

Finally the bed creaked a bit as he laid down, then in a perfect imitation of Hathaway's peculiar way of talking, he said, "Move over, 'ole wommin.' "

Hearing no protest from the "ole wommin," Hathaway jumped up and ran in the bedroom saying, "Stop right war' you 'ere, Bill. The cow is your'n!"

Hathaway's Pet Skunk

Hathaway Jones had a pet skunk. He and his father always had queer pets. They would get them very young and raise them with great care and gentleness. Some of their pets developed intelligence respecting morals, affection, and cleanliness, which might have furnished their masters food for reflection. They frequently converted their wild characteristics into activities which were helpful.

Hathaway's skunk was a civet cat, one of those small spotted animals which, in their natural state, are cold-blooded killers, capable of giving off smells greatly out of proportion with their size. This pet skunk, however, always kept himself clean and sweet-smelling while around the house.

He was raised with the chickens and spent a great deal of his time with them, but he never harmed them. He was very friendly with one old red hen, and cold nights when Hathaway happened to be away from home, she covered him. But, while he never bothered the chickens, he was a good hunter. Every morning he brought Hathaway a pheasant for breakfast.

The Monster Rattler

Version I

One morning Hathaway came running to his grandpap's cabin overlooking the rapids of the Rogue River, excited and all out of breath. Asked by Ike why he was so "het up," he answered that he had killed the biggest rattler in the world.

He said he was walking along the trail above Andy Hatfield's place, and started to step over a small log lying in the trail. Just as he raised his foot, the "log" began to move and Hathaway discovered, "It were one hell-raring big rattler!"

Recovering rapidly from his surprise at seeing such an enormous snake, he shot it through its head a couple of times, finally killing it. While dying, however, the reptile thrashed around so hard it shook off rattles "till they fell round like hail." After the rattler was good and dead, Hathaway picked up rattles until his hat was full, and there were still more than six feet of rattles left on the tail. He swore the snake was 31 feet long, "not countin' the rattles that was shook off."

Version II

Hathaway said he had killed that very morning, just the other side of Clay Hill, the biggest rattlesnake that ever lived. Coming along on his riding mule he noticed a small log across the trail. It was only about eight inches through but his mule refused to approach it. He finally decided the quickest way out would be for him to remove the log, but as he walked toward it he noticed it slowly moving. Then he saw it was a rattlesnake which, due to the cold weather, could only crawl slowly.

He ran back to his riding mule, pulled his rifle out of the boot, returned and shot the snake through the head seven times. The bullets killed the snake, but in dying it thrashed around and scattered rattles all over the hillside. Gathering up the rattles, he soon had his hands full, so he got a two-quart fruit jar from his grub sack and filled it full of rattles, and there were still twenty-seven left on the snake's tail.

The Great Fish Run

One time six men from Portland hired Hathaway Jones to pack them out to High Ridge for deer. They had hired him before upon several trips and knew him quite well. So they decided to start a lying contest and maybe get the best of him.

They began with steelhead fishing, and one man told of the big run of '82, and how he caught enough fish in one afternoon to fill a big smokehouse. Beginning with that for a start, each man in turn added everything he could imagine. The last of the outsiders claimed to have seen a run of steelhead in the lower Rogue which was so great the fish completely covered the bottom of the river, and that thousands were in the air constantly, as far as he could see.

Hathaway listened to their stories, then wished they could see a big run of steelhead. He said it was not at all unusual for the steelhead to be so thick in the water there was no room for the water.

Down the Great Flume

Several years ago an eastern syndicate conducted extensive hydraulic gold mining operations on Grave Creek, a tributary of the eastern reaches of the lower Rogue. A wooden flume twenty miles long was constructed, extending back into the mountains where it connected with an adequate water supply. The fall was great and the flow of the water through the flume was very swift and, being six feet wide and four feet deep, it carried an enormous volume.

Back of the mine the land rose in almost clifflike steepness to an elevation of 400 feet, and upon the top of that formation, the flume ended by union with a thirty-inch steel pipe. From point to point the pipe was reduced until at the "giant," which is a nozzle, it was sixteen inches in diameter. The nozzle was four inches in diameter, but was interchangeable with others of three and two inches. The force of the water from the "giant" was so great it broke up cemented conglomerate as though it were loose gravel. The material was washed down through long sluice boxes which caught and saved the gold.

On one side of the flume throughout its length there was a cat-walk made of two by twelve planks.

During the time the mine was in operation, Hathaway Jones killed a bear near the point back in the mountains where the water entered the flume. It was a small bear, but seeing that it was in good order, he determined to take it home intact, after dressing, of course. However, the distance was great, his cabin being many miles beyond the mine.

Sitting upon a rock while taking a smoke and a rest, he suddenly hit upon what seemed at the time a bright idea. He decided to contrive a small raft, using for that purpose some planks and wire which the builders of the flume had discarded, fasten the bear upon it with wire and float it twenty miles toward home, while he ran beside it along the catwalk.

It required but a short time for him to build the raft which, during its construction, was held in place by a wire fastened to the head of a spike which had not been driven clean into the side of the flume. Having completed the raft satisfactorily, he placed the bear upon it and wired it in place, loosened the wire from the spike, and attempted to jump clear. He had, however, inadvertently wired his foot to the raft. Fortunately his rifle was leaning against the flume and he was able to grab it before the water carried him away.

It was a great ride, and Hathaway, telling about it later, said he enjoyed it even more than he did his ride down a mountain on a snow slide. Around curves, across trestles over deep canyons, and through dark tunnels where the roof was so low he had to stoop in order to clear his head, he sped along with a speed that seemed like flying. He was having such a good time he began singing; then he remembered the pipe

which joined the end of the flume. He realized he was approaching that point with incredible speed.

Rounding a curve, he saw it. Grasping his rifle firmly, he took a deep breath, ducked his head, and dove into the pipe. Hathaway always described his passage through the pipe in his own highly seasoned language but it seemed no time at all until he shot out through the nozzle, holding his rifle, and still on the raft with his bear. The water kicked him, hurtling through the air for 100 feet, dashed him against a rocky wall, slushed and swirled him around, and washed him down through the sluice boxes.

Those were right good sluice boxes. They sluiced Hathaway of all his gold which consisted of a gold crown, three gold fillings, a five dollar gold piece, and the gold bead from the front sight of his rifle, then cast him, his bear, and the raft over the spillway onto the tailings. He then unfastened the wire from around his foot and the bear and walked the rest of the way home. He always said he felt fine after that ride, except for being a little wet.

Hathaway's Marvelous Escape

Version I

Hathaway Jones once set a steel bear trap away back in the mountains where he saw evidence which led him to know there were some big bears living in the neighborhood. Two days later he returned and there was his bear, a monster, caught by the front foot. It was a big brown male, and he shot it through the head, killing it instantly.

He dressed the bear and was getting ready to take it home when here came a great big fat hog, rooting around and grunting now and then. So Hathaway shot the hog, which, after he had dressed it, he judged to weigh 400 pounds. Then, throwing the bear over one shoulder and the hog over the other, he hurried along toward home.

The country through which he was compelled to travel is very rough, steep, and cut with many deep ravines across one of which there was a small log over which he had to walk. He had felled it there a couple of years before. It was a young fir. Down in the bottom of that ravine, forty feet below the log, there was a small stream of water.

Hathaway was always good at walking logs, and even though that one was small and springy, he had walked it several times. But the weight of the game he was carrying caused the log to bend more than usual and right out at the middle a section of bark slipped off, causing him to lose his balance and fall. He landed flat upon his back in the creek between two big boulders. He could not move either arm or his legs, and his nose was just above the surface of the water. It looked like rain, too, and even a small shower would raise the creek a foot or two.

He struggled and heaved but could not move either the hog or the bear, and every time he struggled, his head would go under water. So he ate the hog. It took him three days, but after he got rid of the hog he rolled the bear over, got up, threw it over his shoulder, and went home.

Version II

He killed a bear one day and let's let him tell this one. "I was packing this here bear home on my back" [said Hathaway]. It wasn't a very big one. We was going across this crick on a log and I slipped. The bear went off one side and I went off the other and there we hung. I had him over my shoulders and I couldn't let go and there we hung. It was three weeks we hung and the bear dried out and slipped off on my side."

Hathaway's Marvelous Fall

One nice sunny morning during the "dog days," Hathaway Jones wandered away from home just looking around. He liked to hear the birds sing, the squirrels chatter and bark, and the water rippling down the creeks. He liked to smell the wild flowers and the azaleas in full bloom. Furthermore, at home there was wood to chop and weeds to hoe, chores which could be attended to on cloudy days.

Strolling along whistling at the quail and chattering birds, smelling the flowers and resting here and there, he eventually came to Big Devil's Stairway, a very attractive place to all those who like such places. He enjoyed walking along that narrow slippery trail, while far below the Rogue River roared and rumbled over the rapids.

He was having a fine time until his foot slipped causing

him to lose his balance and fall off the trail. About halfway down he hit something that caused him to bounce, and when he came down he was away across on the other side of the river sitting a-straddle the Devil's Backbone.

Hathaway and the Game Commissioners

Someone reported to the Oregon Game Commission that Hathaway Jones killed old does all the year round and fed them to his dogs; but the name of that very unethical informer has never been known on the Rogue. Everybody in the country fed his dogs on hog and doe. The informer also reported that the local authorities would do nothing about it, seeing that they all fed their own dogs on hog and doe. So the higher-ups sent two bright young city investigators to the lower Rogue on the Hathaway case.

Thinking it would make an impression upon Hathaway, whom the informer had branded as a dangerous killer, a wicked and deadly gun fighter, they decided they would go to his cabin, arrest him, take him to Gold Beach, and there question him.

They had scarcely arrived at Gold Beach before everyone knew what they were and the purpose of their visit, so they were unable to hire anybody to boat them up the river; neither could they hire horses, so they set out on foot carrying some food. They could not even rent a room.

Now Hathaway's cabin was right by the trail, and even before the two young men left Gold Beach, he knew they were coming, it being the custom of the country for such matters to travel fast. About noon of the third day, footsore and weary, they arrived at Hathaway's cabin. He hailed them cheerfully: "Hey thou, pilgrims. Jest in time fer dinner. Come in and rest your feet."

Upon his stove there was a large iron pot full of stew made of the fat shoulder and ribs of a doe, carrots, onions, and potatoes. The young investigators were hungry, so they ate, but in silence. Hathaway waited for them to talk, for that is mountain hospitality. Finally one of the young fellows told Hathaway that they were game commissioners, that he was under arrest, and that he would have to go with them to Gold Beach.

They told him he might be gone for a long time, so he went about putting his house in order. Finished with all else, he decided to throw the shells out of his Winchester so the spring in the chamber would not be weakened. By that time he had become annoyed, and was mumbling a few cuss words. He grabbed up his rifle, began ejecting the shells, and right there the nerves of those young city investigators cracked.

Away they went down the trail on the run with Hathaway right after them, calling for them to wait for him. He chased them clear to Gold Beach, yelling and swearing at them every time they showed signs of giving out. He caught them at the courthouse, but all they could say was: "Please, don't shoot." Hathaway handed them their hats which they had forgotten in their hurry and invited them to stop in any time they were passing his way.

NOTES
to "The Münchausen of the Rogue"

1. Jan Harold Brunvand, *The Study of American Folklore* (New York, 1968), p.93.

2. For the history of the exploration, settlement, and Indian wars in the region see Stephen Dow Beckham, *Requiem For a People: The Rogue Indians and the Frontiersmen,* Civilization of the American Indian Series, vol. 108 (Norman, Okla.: University of Oklahoma Press, 1971).

3. *Genealogical Material in Oregon Donation Land Claims: Abstracts From Applications Filed in Roseburg, The Dalles and La-Grande Land Offices,* Genealogical Material in Oregon Donation Land Claims, vol. 3 (Portland, Ore.: Genealogical Forum of Portland, Oregon, Inc., 1962), p.52. A. G. Walling, *History of Southern Oregon* (Portland, Ore.: A. G. Walling, Printer, 1884), p.513.

4. *Roseburg Review,* Dec. 10, 1893; *Roseburg Plaindealer,* Dec. 10, 1893.

5. The other children of the marriage included: William Burr Jones, born March 3, 1864; Albert Duane Jones, born Oct. 23, 1868; Clare Ellen Jones, born Oct. 10, 1871; Rupert Leslie Jones, born June 23, 1873; Katherine Hermia Jones, born July 18, 1875; Dedrick Eusted Jones, born March 20, 1880; and Claus Lewellyn Jones, born March 24, 1881. William S. Jones Bible, in possession of Claus L. "Todd" Jones, Powers, Ore. Claus L. Jones, Interview by J. Curtis Beckham, Nov. 8, 1970, Powers, Ore., MS notes in possession of author.

6. U. S. Census, 1880, Deer Creek Precinct, Douglas County, Ore., Microcopy T-9, National Archives, Washington, D. C. Claus L. Jones, Interview by J. Curtis Beckham, Aug. 24, 1971, Powers, Ore., MS notes in possession of author.

7. Claude Riddle, *In the Happy Hills* (Roseburg, Ore., 1954), p.1.

8. *Ibid.*

9. Beckham, *Requiem,* p.171. "Miscellaneous Records," vol. 2, Clerk's Office, Curry County Courthouse, Gold Beach, Ore., p.23.

10. *Gold Beach Gazette,* June 15, 1886.

11. L. M. Lowell, "Roseburg (Douglas County)," MS, File II-B, Box 66-9, WPA Oregon Historical Records Survey, University of Oregon, Eugene, Ore.

12. *Gold Beach Gazette,* March 8, 1895. Ethel M. Claxton, "Oak Flat Illahe (Big Bend), Agness," MS, File VII-C, Box 66-7, WPA Oregon Historical Records Survey, University of Oregon, Eugene, Ore. Henry Teller Price, *Up the Rogue River and the First Mail Route* (Portland, Ore.: Metropolitan Press, 1967).

13. *Portland Oregonian,* Sept. 23, 1937. Claus L. Jones Interview, Aug. 24, 1971.

14. Claxton, "Oak Flat."

15. Richard M. Dorson, *American Folklore* (Chicago, 1959), p.227.

16. Nancy Wilson Ross, *Farthest Reach: Oregon & Washington* (New York, 1941), p.299.

17. *Portland Oregonian,* Sept. 26, 1937.

18. This thesis is explored in Brunvand, *American Folklore,* pp.115–116.

19. Ross, *Farthest Reach,* pp.300–301.

20. Arthur Dorn, "Folklore: Lower Rogue River," Box 65, Series 1, WPA Oregon Folklore Project, Oregon State Library, Salem, Ore.

21. Ross, *Farthest Reach,* p.300.

22. Riddle, *Happy Hills,* p.5.

23. Jean Muir, "The Hermits Who Hate Hollywood," *Saturday Evening Post* (Feb. 9, 1946), p.27.

24. Riddle, *Happy Hills,* p.1.

25. Mody Boatright, *Folk Laughter on the American Frontier* (New York: 1949), p.88.

26. Sadie and Charles Pettinger, Interview by Alice Wooldridge, Dec. 24, 1967, Arago, Ore., MS notes in possession of author.

27. Linda Barker, "Hathaway Jones," MS, Randall V. Mills Folklore Archive, University of Oregon, Eugene, Ore.

28. *Portland Oregonian,* Sept. 23, 1937.

29. Ross, *Farthest Reach,* p.299.

30. Addie Fitzhugh Helmkin, Interview by Stephen Dow Beckham, March 25, 1972, Sixes River, Ore. John Fitzhugh, "The Beckoning Hand," MS in possession of author.

31. Addie Fitzhugh Helmkin Interview, March 25, 1972.

32. Helene Ashley, "An Anecdote of John Fitzhugh As Told by Fred S. Moore," File XIV-E, Box 66-7, WPA Oregon Historical Records Survey, University of Oregon, Eugene, Ore.

33. Dorn, "Folklore: Lower Rogue River." Orvil O. Dodge, *Pioneer History of Coos and Curry Counties, Oregon* (Salem, Ore.: Capitol Printing Company, 1898), Biographical Appendix, p.22. Edith Fry Smith, Interview by Arthur Dorn, March 27, 1941, Agness, Ore., Box 66, WPA Oregon Writer's Project, Oregon State Library, Salem, Ore.

34. Edith Fry Smith Interview, March 27, 1941. Dorn, "Folklore: Lower Rogue River."

35. "Historical Sketch of Curry County," File I-A & B, Box 66-7, WPA Historical Records Survey, University of Oregon, Eugene, Ore.

36. Dorn, "Folklore: Lower Rogue River."

NOTES AND SOURCES

Almost all the yarns of Hathaway Jones are classifiable as "Tales of Lying," types 1875–1899 in the Aarne-Thompson and Baughman indexes, in particular the cycle known as "Münchausen Tales" and subdivided under type 1889. The following notes call attention to the motifs rather than the types of these lying tales, since the motifs are more diversified.

THE ADVENTURES OF IKE JONES

Ike Jones and the Smart Bear

This tale is a variant of X1221(f), "Bears: miscellaneous," and X1233, "Lies about hogs." It has similarities to the Ozark tale recounted by Vance Randolph in *We Always Lie to Strangers* (New York, 1951), p.34, which Baughman lists as X1233(ag), "Bear tries to fatten razorback hogs by penning them up, feeding them corn. The bear gives up, turns the hogs loose."
Source: Dorn Collection.

Ike Jones and the Rattlesnakes

The tale is a new variant of X1321.2, "Large number of snakes." The introduction of "venom vapor" is a unique refinement that adds ludicrous plausibility to a most unusual event. Baughman locates nine varieties of this motif, but they all relate to snakes in a single den. The tale contains the generational confusion, making Ike the father of Hathaway.
Informant: John Fry, who said he heard the tale from Ike Jones. Dorn Collection.

Ike's Maple Shoe Pegs

Motif X1822*, "Lie: shoe pegs sold for oats." Mody Boatright collected this same tale in the Gib Morgan repertoire. In that rendering the pegs are shipped by barge to St. Louis where a strike of shoeworkers makes it impossible to sell the pegs; they are sold for oats. Boatright, *Gib Morgan: Minstrel of the Oil Fields* (Dallas, 1945), pp.85–86. This particular tale is given more than usual detail by exact dating, trail description, and even the offhand mention that the adventurers spent the night near "the mission" carving down the pegs.

Informant: probably John Fry. Dorn Collection.

Ike Jones and the Great Rattler

Motif X1321.1.1, "Remarkably long snake," is a sub-element in the tale. The account is a new variant on X1321.4.1*, "Ferocious snake." The understatement of the tale's last line puzzles and delights the listener. In this account the generation confusion makes Hathaway the son of Ike.

Informant: Hathaway Jones. Dorn Collection.

Ike Jones's Woodpecker

The tale is a new variant of motif X1269*, "Lies about woodpeckers," and introduces a refinement to B210, "Speaking animals"; Solomon III not only talks but sings hymns. 1086.1*, "Lie; ingenious man uses animal in construction work," is the closest motif in Baughman to the labors of the woodpeckers in this tale. Prairie dogs helped Pecos Bill dig fence postholes; gophers performed the same labor for Paul Bunyan; having birds do agricultural labor is a new departure.

Informant: Hathaway Jones. Dorn Collection.

Ike Jones and Lucifer

This tale contains a variety of detail to enhance its credibility. The informant, John Fry, said that he knew Mary Harkness, the

child carried away by the panther. It is a new variant of X1213, "Lies about panthers," and contains the motif B520, "Animals save person's life."
Informant: John Fry. Dorn Collection.

Ike's Raven, "Lemuel"

Several motifs appear in the tale. Two from the B300–599 classification, "Friendly Animals," are B520, "Animals save person's life," and B210, "Speaking animals." This latter motif is especially relevant in that it follows Baughman's guideline that the speech of the animal becomes the point of the joke. "Lemuel" leaves no doubt about this! The tale is as well a variant on X1252, "Lies about crows," and has affinities to X1207*, "Lie: animals are trained to dig (or do other work) for construction boss."
Informant: probably John Fry. Dorn Collection.

Ike Jones Calls the Hogs

The tale is a new variant on motif X1124, "Lie: the hunter catches or kills game by ingenious or unorthodox method." Baughman finds twelve variants; none is similar to Ike Jones's remarkable hog calling. Interestingly the account finishes in a tone of understatement and introduces motif J2160, "Other short-sighted acts."
Informant: Claude Bardin, Dec. 8, 1940. Dorn Collection.

Misadventures of Ike Jones

Several accounts remembered as "Hathaway Jones stories" are more anecdotal than developed tales. Arthur Dorn considered these, however, part of the Jones repertoire. The affinity of this particular tale to the Münchausen genre is clear; Ike Jones was a miller at Roseburg not an absent-minded resident of Rogue River. Elements of the general motif J2000, "Absurd absent-mindedness," are present.
Informant: Claude Bardin, Dec. 8, 1940. Dorn Collection.

The Two-Headed Snake

Recounted in an anecdotal manner by Rogue River pioneer Andrew J. Hatfield, the tale contains motif X1321, "Extraordinary snakes." It is a new variant.
Source: Andrew J. Hatfield, June 12, 1941. Dorn Collection.

The Wild Hog Derby

Arthur Dorn considerably embellished this anecdotal account of the late nineteenth century. The plausibility of the events are such that the tale is perhaps about an actual event. The Frys, Billings, and Walker all lived in the canyon in the 1880's. A possible motif is X1233(gj), "Fast running hogs."
Source: John Fry, Feb. 23, 1941. Dorn Collection.

THE ADVENTURES OF SAMPSON JONES

The Birth and Childhood of Sampson Jones

Although clearly a Münchausen tale, this story has elements of type 301, "The Three Stolen Princesses," in that the strong hero is suckled by an animal. A variety of motifs are introduced: X912(h), "Hero grows up with animals"; X912(d), "Food of hero in childhood"; B211.1, "Speaking beasts"; and B292, "Animal in service of man." One of the most important motifs, however, is X1213, "Lies about panthers," of which this is a new variant.
Source: Dorn Collection.

The Flat World of Sampson Jones

This account is one of the few in the Jones cycles that is not readily identified as a lying tale. It suggests motif J1930, "Absurd disregard of natural laws."
Source: Dorn Collection.

Sampson's Deer Jerky

This tale has an evident anecdotal element in it, but it possesses affinities to J1190, "Cleverness in the law court: miscellaneous." Adding an assurance of plausibility, the story's teller, Rolly Canfield, said that he attended the trial many years ago.

Informant: Rolly Canfield, Nov. 22, 1940. Dorn Collection.

THE ADVENTURES OF HATHAWAY JONES

The Big Potato Crop

Motif X1435(a), "Remarkable potato hill." The tale has implications of motif X1532, "Rich soil produces remarkable crop," though such was apparently not Jones's point of emphasis. This version is almost identical with motif X1435(aa), "Man digs into potato hill; thirty-seven bushels run out before he can plug up the hole." Baughman found the variant in Esther Shephard, *Paul Bunyan* (New York, 1941), pp.64–67. Within the tale is the recurrent rendering of the "remarkable carrier," motif X942. Nancy Wilson Ross in *Farthest Reach: Oregon & Washington* (New York, 1941), p.299, gives the tale in fragment. Robert D. Hume, the "salmon king," operated canneries at the river's mouth from 1883 until his death in 1907.

Source: Dorn Collection.

Hathaway's Melons

X1402.1*(ab), "Melons provided with carts so they do not wear out," was collected in Missouri by Vance Randolph. See *We Always Lie to Strangers* (New York, 1951), p.90.

Source: Dorn Collection.

The Watermelon Money

Motif X903, "Lie used as a catch tale." This tale is both biographical and humorous. Its opening may indicate some Münchausen elements; they are, however, not developed in this version.

Source: Dorn Collection.

NOTES AND SOURCES

The Raccoon Tree

The tale is a new variant of X1249.4*, "Lies about racoons," and of X1124, "Lie: the hunter catches or kills game by ingenious or unorthodox method." Warren S. Walker collected a similar tale, X1249.4*(b), "Hollow tree full of raccoons; man shoots them from the bottom hole; they roll out, one by one; the man has a wagon-load of raccoons." *Midwest Folklore,* IV (1954), 154.

Sources. Version I: Larry Lucas, Aug. 18, 1968. Beckham Collection. Version II: Dorn Collection, Feb. 14, 1941.

The Slow Bullet

Two motifs appear: X1121.3*, "Lie: remarkable ammunition used by great hunter," and a variant on X1759*(gd), "Man shoots at deer; he goes back next day, starts to shoot at deer; just as he aims, the bullet shot previous day hits and kills deer." Halpert collected the tale in the John Darling cycles, *JAF,* LVII (1944), 102.

Sources. Version I: Dorn Collection. Version II: Hathaway Jones. Dorn Collection.

The Remarkable Bullet

Baughman classifies the "Lucky Shot: Miscellaneous Forms," as properly a Münchausen tale. Motif X1121.3*, "Lie: remarkable ammunition used by great hunter." See Baron Münchausen, *The Adventures of Baron Münchausen* (New York, 1944), p.136.

Sources. Version I: Larry Lucas, August 18, 1968. Beckham Collection. Version II: Kathryn McPherson, "Hathaway Jones, Rogue's Paul Bunyan," *Oregon's South Coast* (Coos Bay, Ore., 1960). Version III: Dorn Collection, Dec. 15, 1940.

Old Betsy's Remarkable Shot

The tale is similar to Jones's slow-bullet stories while hunting for deer. It is a new variant of X1759*(g), "Absurd disregard of the nature of gunpowder."

Informant: Hathaway Jones. Dorn Collection.

Hathaway's Poor Marksmanship

The tale is a familiar one. Motif X1123*, "Lie: poor marksmanship. Hunter shoots at a flock of birds with large shotgun. His aim is low, but he picks up a basketful (or sackful) of toenails or birdlegs." The Jones refinement is a basketful of bills. B. A. Botkin in *A Treasury of American Folklore* (New York, 1944), p.281, gives the version of Henry Hawley in whose yarn the hunter collected four and one-half bushels of wild pigeons' feet and legs. See also H. W. Thompson, *Body, Boots and Britches* (Philadelphia, 1939), p.295.

Informants. Version I: Glen Wooldridge, who told it to Jean Muir. Muir, "The Hermits Who Hate Hollywood," *Saturday Evening Post,* Feb. 9, 1946. Version II: Larry Lucas, Aug. 18, 1968. Beckham Collection.

The Hunting Hound

New variant of X1215.10, "Lie: dog with remarkable scent." C. S. Barnett published a similar tale in *American Stuff* (New York, 1937), p.55. Baughman X1215.10(a), "Farmer stores block of ice with raccoon tracks on it. The next July he takes the block from the ice house to make ice cream. The dog sniffs the ice, has the raccoon up a tree in half an hour."

Informant: Ed Troyer, June 26, 1967. Beckham Collection.

Towser and Nellie

This tale was evidently one of Arthur Dorn's favorites in the varied Jones repertoire. He described it at length in December, 1940, to Claire Churchill, head of Oregon's WPA folklore project. It has motif X1215.13*, "Lie: remarkable dog, miscellaneous."

Informant: Hathaway Jones, who told it to Dorn about 1925 at the Agness boat landing. Dorn Collection.

The Flying Bear

The catch-tale element of this account is only partially developed. The motifs include: X903, "Lie used as a catch tale"; X133, "Lie:

the hunter in danger"; X1221(c), "Ferocious bear"; and a new variant on X1741.8*, "Disregard of gravity, miscellaneous."
Source: Dorn Collection.

Hathaway Out-Climbs the Bear

Motif K657, "Exaggerated tales about escapes," is relevant. Vardis Fisher in *Idaho Lore* (Caldwell, Ida., 1939), p.136, recounted another bear-and-hunter-in-tree escape tale but with distinct differences. Other motifs include X1133, "Lie: the hunter in danger"; X1221(c), "Ferocious bear"; and X1830*, "Tall tales about escapes."
Informant: Claude Bardin. Dorn Collection.

The Bear Hunt

See note to "Hathaway Out-Climbs the Bear." Motifs X1133, "Lie: the hunter in danger"; X1221(c). "Ferocious bear"; X1830*, "Tall tales about escapes"; and K657, "Exaggerated tales about escapes." Baldy Criteser was Hathaway's cousin and a long-time wilderness resident on Rogue River. His father, Thompson Criteser, assumed management of the Roseburg Flouring Mills when Isaac Jones was too old to run the business. Baldy lived at Paradise Bar. His wife, Mae Cain Criteser, died in August, 1929, and was buried at Paradise next to the Rogue River Trail.
Source: Dorn Collection.

The Bear and the Honey Tree

The tale is a new variant of X1124, "Lie: the hunter catches or kills game by an ingenious or unorthodox method." It has strong affinities to X1124(d), "Man bores holes in tree trunk, fills them with honey. He hangs heavy stone in front of the holes. A bear pushes rock away to get at honey; the rock hits him in head; he pushes it harder; it hits him harder. This continues until stone knocks his brains out." See Robert E. Gard, *Johnny Chinoock: Tall Tales and True from the Canadian West* (London, 1945), p.203.
Informant: Sam Baer, June 26, 1967. Beckham Collection.

The Bear and the Bees

An unidentifiable motif appears in this tale: the making of a loud noise that causes bees to swarm. The story introduces a new variant of X1221, "Lies about bears," which is similar to X1221(aa), "Bear is so large that hunter gets seven barrels of bear oil from it." See Stan Newton, *Paul Bunyan of the Great Lakes* (New York, 1946), p.147.
Source: Dorn Collection.

The Two Hungry Bears

Motifs X1221(f), "Bears: miscellaneous"; and a new variant of X1741.1, "Person or animal rises into the air in defiance of gravity."
Sources. Version I: Sam Baer, June 26, 1967. Beckham Collection. Version II: Allen, "Tall Tales from Oregon's Red [sic] River Country," *Geological Society of the Oregon Country Newsletter*, IX (Jan. 10, 1943), 6.

The Trials of Hathaway

Typical of the Jones tales, this one contains several motifs. Central perhaps is J1874, "Relieving the beast of burden." Other elements include: X942(a), "Person carries animals"; X1242, "Lies about mules"; and a variation on X1221(aa), "Bear is so large that hunter gets seven barrels of bear oil from it." The Linda Barker manuscript, University of Oregon, contains only the fragment on the size of the bear—it yielded twenty gallons of grease.
Informants. Version I: Glen Wooldridge, who told it to Jean Muir. Muir, "The Hermits Who Hate Hollywood," *Saturday Evening Post*, Feb. 9, 1946. Version II: Loson Winn. Winn, "Hathaway Jones: Teller of Tall Tales," *Pioneer Days in Canyonville*, I (August, 1968), 38.

Independent Mules

New variant of motif X1242(d), "Remarkable mule: miscellaneous."

Sources. Version I: McPherson, "Hathaway Jones, Rogue's Paul Bunyan," *Oregon's South Coast* (Coos Bay, Ore., 1960). Version II: Dorn Collection, March 21, 1941.

Hathaway's Old Mule

The tale is anecdotal and may likely represent an actual event and comment. Tentative motif, X100, "Humor of disability."
Source: Dorn Collection.

Hathaway's Worthless Mule

New variant of motif X1242(d), "Remarkable mule: miscellaneous."
Source: Ed Troyer and Sam Baer, June 26, 1967. Beckham Collection.

Hathaway's Remarkable Mule

Mules were an everyday part of life for Hathaway. They were "almost" human in his view. This tale has two new variants of X1242(d), "Remarkable mule: miscellaneous," and X1741.8*, "Disregard of gravity: miscellaneous." Usually this latter motif has appeared in tales about marvelous leaps to great heights or stepping out of a deadly fall.
Source: Dorn Collection.

The Red-Hot Mule

The tale contains motif X1242(b), "Fast mule," but it is a new variant. Baughman gives X1242(ba), "Mule pulls plow so fast that owner hitches him to two plows. The friction from one burns up the earth." This tale was published in 1878 in Fred H. Hart, *The Sazerac Lying Club* (San Francisco), p.204.
Source: Dorn Collection.

The Hot Weather

The tale is a new variant of X1633, "Lie: effect of heat on animals."
Sources. Version I: Sam Baer, June 26, 1967. Beckham Collection.

Version II: Larry Lucas, Aug. 18, 1968. Beckham Collection. Version III: Dorn Collection.

The Year of the Big Freeze

The tale introduces a variety of motifs and new variants. It is very similar to X1606.2.4*, "Wild fowl are frozen into ice when they jump into water just as quick hard freeze hits," published by Boyce House in *Tall Talk from Texas* (San Antonio, Tex., 1944), p.12. Other elements include: X1737, "Man stays under water for long period of time"; X1303.1, "Big fish pulls man or boat"; and X1303.3*, "Remarkable leap of big fish." The account concludes with the Stith Thompson motif D441.7, "Transformation: sticks of wood to animals." Intense freezes are very unusual in western Oregon. In 1925 and 1972 the Siuslaw River froze over in its upper tidewater reaches; swifter streams, such as the Rogue, seldom have much ice.

Informant: Lin Blondell, Dec. 23, 1940.

The Great Snow

Baughman found ten variants of motif X1653.3, "Deep snow." Hathaway's new variant is more heroic than any so far indicated. In New York and Minnesota are tales of animals stepping into chimneys (see Baughman, X1653.3(bb)), but nothing contains a hero who can walk thirty miles beneath the snow's surface and emerge to scare an old Indian woman.

Source: Dorn Collection.

The Lost Bacon and the Deep Snow

Jones had several tales about the great snow depth in the Rogue wilderness. This particular one is a new variant of X1653.3, "Deep snow."

Source: Dorn Collection.

The Devil's Stairway

Motif X1733.1, "Man lifts heavy load, sinks into solid rock." Baughman identifies twelve variants; of these four of motif X1733.2* have close affinity to this tale. The distribution of the tale is strongly northern. It has been collected in Vermont, Wisconsin, New Jersey, and Indiana–Illinois. William H. Jansen identifies sixteen variants of it in the repertoire of Abraham "Oregon" Smith. See Jansen, "Abraham 'Oregon' Smith," Ph.D. dissertation, Indiana University, 1949.

Source: Dorn Collection.

The Broken Leg

The hazards of Rogue River life are revealed in this none-too-fictional account. Jones confronts danger and renders it harmless in a lighthearted yarn. The story is a new variant of X1012, "Lie: person displays remarkable ingenuity or resourcefulness."

Source: Dorn Collection.

Hathaway's Great Strength

Although a Münchausen tale, this story's leading of the listener to a particular question places it in the catch-tale tradition. It is a variant of X940, "Lie: person of remarkable strength." The introduction of biographical detail about Hathaway illustrates the evolution of one of his stories from an account by him into an account about him.

Source: Dorn Collection.

Gold in the Far Country

The absurdity of this tale's last line is its most memorable and durable feature. Some informants had forgotten the tale and remembered only the closing phrase. It is a new variant of X1818.1*, "Tall tales about rich ore."

Sources. Version I: Sam Baer, June 26, 1967. Beckham Collection. Version II: Larry Lucas, Aug. 18, 1968. Beckham Collection.

Hathaway's Rich Lode

The tale is a new variant of X1818.1*, "Tall tales about rich ore," and has similarities to X1818.1*(e), "Veins of gold are so rich that on warm days the gold oozes out of crevices in cliffs." This version was collected in California, Wayland D. Hand, *California Folklore Quarterly*, I (1942), 153.

Sources: Version I: Hathaway Jones. Claude Riddle, "In the Hills with Hathaway," *In the Happy Hills* (Roseburg, Ore., 1954). Version II: McPherson, "Hathaway Jones, Rogue's Paul Bunyan," *Oregon's South Coast* (Coos Bay, Ore., 1960). Version III: Dorn Collection.

The Remarkable Watch

The tale is nearly identical to X1755.1(c), "Watch lost for six months is found by owner on return trip. Watch is keeping perfect time." See Dorothy J. Baylor, *Hoosier Folklore*, VI (1947), 98. The lesser motif is X1653.3, "Deep snow."

Sources. Version I: McPherson, "Hathaway Jones, Rogue's Paul Bunyan," *Oregon's South Coast* (Coos Bay, Ore., 1960). Version II: Arthur Dorn. Ross, *Farthest Reach: Oregon & Washington* (New York, 1941). Version III: Joel Barker. Barker, "Hathaway Jones," MS, Randall V. Mills Folklore Archive, University of Oregon, Eugene, Ore. Version IV: Hathaway Jones. Dorn Collection.

The Magnificent Fireplace

The tale is a variant of X1767.2*, "Absurd disregard for nature of drafts." Richard M. Dorson found a similar yarn, X1767.2*(a), "Draft draws wood out of stove, up chimney," in Vermont. Dorson, *Jonathan Draws the Long Bow: New England Popular Tales and Legends* (Cambridge, Mass., 1946), p.258. Chester Smith located it in New York, "Henry Brown, Storyteller of the Highlands," *New York Folklore Quarterly*, V (1949), 63. Jones's version has had a remarkable popularity in southern Oregon. It is preserved in several accounts with minor detail variation.

Sources. Version I: Hathaway Jones. Riddle, "In the Hills with Hathaway," *In the Happy Hills* (Roseburg, Ore., 1954). Version II: Joel Barker. Barker, "Hathaway Jones," MS, Randall V. Mills Folklore Archive, University of Oregon, Eugene, Ore. Version III: Dorn

Collection. Version IV: Loson Winn. Winn, "Hathaway Jones: Teller of Tall Tales," *Pioneer Days in Canyonville*, I (August, 1968), 38.

The Rolling Stone

The tale is a new variant of motif X1747*, "Object behaves without regard for natural friction." It has similarities to X1747*(a), "Man slides hickory log down mountainside. It comes down with such force that it climbs mountain on other side of valley. It slides back and forth so long that it wears down to toothpick size." Vance Randolph found two versions: one produced a toothpick; the other made a ramrod. See *We Always Lie to Strangers* (New York, 1951), p.20. The Jones tale appears in summary in *Oregon, End of the Trail* (Portland, 1940), p.82.

Sources. Version I: Arthur Dorn. Ross, *Farthest Reach: Oregon & Washington* (New York, 1941). Version II: Sam Baer and Ed Troyer, June 26, 1967. Beckham Collection. Version III: McPherson, "Hathaway Jones, Rogue's Paul Bunyan," *Oregon's South Coast* (Coos Bay, Ore., 1960). Version IV: Allen, "Tall Tales from Oregon's Red [sic] River County," *Geological Society of the Oregon Country Newsletter*, IX (Feb. 25, 1943), 25. Version V: Hathaway Jones. Dorn Collection.

The Seven-Foot Bread Loaf

Baughman identifies the motif X1811.1, "Lie, the giant loaf of bread," but cites no examples.

Source: McPherson, "Hathaway Jones, Rogue's Paul Bunyan," *Oregon's South Coast* (Coos Bay, Ore., 1960).

Ticks in the Rogue Wilderness

Baughman provides no appropriate motif. Perhaps this tale can be viewed as a new variant of X1297.1*, "Remarkable tick." One version has altered the tale to be about fleas rather than ticks.

Sources. Version I: Dorn Collection. Version II: Hathaway Jones.

Riddle, "In the Hills with Hathaway," *In the Happy Hills* (Roseburg, Ore., 1954).

The Cow and the "Ole Wommin"

This tale may be an anecdote. It does, however, possess threads of a Münchausen theme. A possible motif is X100, "Humor of disability."

Source: McPherson, "Hathaway Jones, Rogue's Paul Bunyan," *Oregon's South Coast* (Coos Bay, Ore., 1960).

Hathaway's Pet Skunk

The tale is a new variant of X1124, "Lie: the hunter catches or kills game by ingenious or unorthodox method."

Source: Claude Bardin, Nov. 26, 1940. Dorn Collection.

The Monster Rattler

Two distinct but related motifs are evident: X1321.1.1, "Remarkably long snake," and X1321.1.2, "Great snake is thought to be a log." One Louisiana tale produced a near rival to the snake in size—a rattler twenty-two feet long with twenty-five rattles. Masterson, *Journal of American Folklore*, LIX (1946), 174.

Sources. Version I: McPherson, "Hathaway Jones, Rogue's Paul Bunyan," *Oregon's South Coast* (Coos Bay, Ore., 1960). Version II: Dorn Collection.

The Great Fish Run

Hathaway could swap yarns with anyone on the trail; occasionally his tales got him involved in the "contest in lying." The obvious motif is X905, "Lying contests," with the lesser motif X1317, "Crowded fish," carrying the story interest. Baughman reports several variants of which X1317.1*, "Fish are so thick in stream that people cross stream on backs of fish without wetting feet," has a near content similarity. Dorson reports this motif in *Journal of American Folklore*, XLVIII (1945), 106.

Source: Dorn Collection.

NOTES AND SOURCES

Down the Great Flume

This account makes appropriate use of the once ambitious gold mining enterprises of the Rogue wilderness. It contains motif X1830*, "Tall tales about escapes."
Informant: Claude Bardin. Dorn Collection.

Hathaway's Marvelous Escape

The tale, preserved in two rather divergent accounts, contains several motif elements. They include: X931, "Lie: remarkable eater," with special variation on X931(ei), "Man eats whole bear," wherein a man was trapped in a cave by a bear he had killed at its entrance; he had to eat his way to freedom. See Randolph, *We Always Lie to Strangers* (New York, 1951), p. 109. Also present are new variants of X942(a), "Person carries animals," and X1133, "Lie: the hunter in danger."
Source. Version I: Claude Bardin. Dorn Collection. Version II: Joel Barker, "Hathaway Jones," MS, Randall V. Mills Folklore Archive, University of Oregon, Eugene, Ore.

Hathaway's Marvelous Fall

The tale is incomplete or not fully developed. The opening is unusual, but the transition to the spectacular event of the account is missing. Tragically Hathaway died in a fall that left his lifeless body on the rocks below the trail at Flea Creek. Motif X1731, "Lies about falling."
Source: Dorn Collection.

Hathaway and the Game Commissioners

The tale was recounted in 1940 by George Rilea, long-time postmaster of Agness. While the account has an anecdotal quality, the "windy" nature reveals itself near the tale's conclusion. A possible motif is X1850, "Other tall tales."
Informant: George Rilea, Nov. 21, 1940. Dorn Collection.

BIBLIOGRAPHY

Indexes and Reference Works

Aarne, Antti, and Thompson, Stith. *The Types of the Folktale: A Classification and Bibliography.* FF Communications No. 184. Helsinki: Suomalainen Tiedeakatemia Academia Scientiarium Fennica, 1961.

Baughman, Ernest W. *Type and Motif-Index of the Folktales of England and North America.* Indiana University Folklore Series No. 20. The Hague: Mouton & Co., 1966.

Boatright, Mody. *Folk Laughter on the American Frontier.* New York: Collier, 1949.

Brunvand, Jan Harold. *The Study of American Folklore: An Introduction.* New York: W. W. Norton & Company, Inc., 1968.

Chase, Richard. *American Folk Tales and Songs.* New York: New American Library, 1956.

Dorson, Richard M. *American Folklore.* Chicago: University of Chicago Press, 1959.

Funk and Wagnalls Standard Dictionary of Folklore, Mythology and Legend. New York: Funk & Wagnalls Company, 1949.

Henningsen, Gustav. "The Art of Perpendicular Lying." Translated by Warren E. Roberts. *Journal of the Folklore Institute* 2: 180–219.

Rourke, Constance. *American Humor: A Study of the National Character.* New York: Harcourt, Brace and Company, Inc., 1931.

Thompson, Stith. *Motif–Index of Folk Literature.* 6 vols. Bloomington: Indiana University Press, 1955–58.

Collections

Barker, Linda. "Hathaway Jones," MS, Randall V. Mills Folklore Archives, University of Oregon, Eugene, Ore.

[177]

BIBLIOGRAPHY

Beckham, Stephen Dow. "Tales of Hathaway Jones: Interviews with Larry Lucas, Sam Baer, Ed Troyer, John Pettinger, and Mary Reitsma," MS in possession of author.

Dorn, Arthur. "Folklore: Lower Rogue River," WPA Oregon Folklore Project, Oregon State Library, Salem, Ore.

McPherson, Kathryn. "Hathaway Jones, Rogue's Paul Bunyan." *Oregon's South Coast.* Coos Bay, Ore.: The World Publishing Company, 1960.

Muir, Jean. "The Hermits Who Hate Hollywood." *Saturday Evening Post,* Feb. 9, 1946, pp.26–27, 71 ff.

Riddle, Claude. "In the Hills With Hathaway," *In the Happy Hills: A Story of Early Day Deer Hunting.* Roseburg, Ore.: M-M Printers, 1954.

Ross, Nancy Wilson. *Farthest Reach: Oregon & Washington.* New York: Alfred A. Knopf, 1941.

Winn, Loson. "Hathaway Jones: Teller of Tall Tales," *Pioneer Days in Canyonville* 1(1968), 37.

———. "Another 'Hathaway' Story," *Pioneer Days in Canyonville* 2(1969), 18.